The House at the End of the Lane

The House at the End of the Lane

story   *pictures*
Elizabeth Rush · Sarah Wilson

A Star & Elephant Book

1982

A Star & Elephant Book
from The Green Tiger Press
La Jolla · California 92038

First Edition · First Printing
Paperbound ISBN 0-914676-64-4

For all of us

Contents

A List of Colored Plates

Maps

At the back of the book there is a fold-out map of the House
at the End of the Lane and the grounds.

The House at the End of the Lane

Chapter 1
The Rescue

He walked down the road in the black night, staying in the very middle, for he was afraid of what might be lurking, crouched there in the bushes or in the tall grass. It wasn't easy to keep going along the road, but on the other hand if he thought about it, there was just as much darkness behind him.

His soft feet made very little noise at all, and as he walked, and walked, and walked, his steps became slower, and slower, and yet slower still, until he stopped, and sat down to rest. His head hung down and his eyes were like two glasses of water ready to spill. Then the bushes moved some few feet away, and sounds made by a large animal came from a fence near the road. He was so tired and homeless, the stars were so far away, and now he heard these noises!

"Goodness, what was that?"

His breath began going faster, his eyes opened wider, trying to see into the darkness. He was so frightened he started to run without thinking. Down the road he ran, away from the place of fright; faster, quicker, each foot up, and down, and-a-hop, up, and down, and-a-hop. After a mile or so he grew so heavy with tiredness that his feet stopped running and just walked; then they stopped walking, and he sat down on a rock under a tree beside the road. He sat and cried, because he was so tired, and so hungry. But the largest tears, the ones that hurt his heart, were the ones that slipped down his cheeks because he was alone.

He leaned against the tree behind him, closed his eyes to squeeze away the last of the tears. Suddenly a snuffling began, almost touch-close. He hopped up and started to run again, but in his fright, he fell, hit his head, and knew nothing.

The snuffling came closer, and a decided stomping accompanied the sound.

"Gracious goodness, what's this? Why—the poor fellow, he's hit his head. I must take him home at once."

When Bartholomew awoke the next morning he could hardly believe where he seemed to be. Never was a kangaroo so comfortable! For never was a bed so soft, nor sheets so sweet to smell or so comforting to the aches he had all over. Quickly he snapped shut his eyes, and bunched them together tight in the middle, and held himself water-still. He was thinking that he must keep this dream, for it was such a lovely dream.

He would probably have been there for hours, holding fast to that dream, if there hadn't been a peculiar noise, The repeated sound was not close, nor was it like anything he had ever heard.

"Glumble-glumble-glumble."

"There, it stopped," Bartholomew thought, as he lay there with his eyes shut, but then came a crash. Bartholomew was wondering so intently what could possibly make such a noise, that one of his eyes opened wide, and then of course there was no trying to pretend any longer. He was quite awake, so he might as well open the other eye. What a lovable, funny kangaroo he was, as he sat there in bed being so pleased with everything, his two round black eyes swinging from side to side like a pendulum, trying to see everything at once. In the fireplace a happy fire was eating a noisy breakfast of dry sycamore logs. On a long oval table near the seat under the

windows was a bowl of the most beautiful flowers he had ever seen, all yellow and a-shine. They were sitting like tiny birds all along the stems, nodding hello, making him feel so good he hopped out of bed and pattered over to touch them.

He had looked out of the window just long enough to notice that he was on the top storey of a tall stone house, when a tiny tapping began at the door. He ran back to the bed, jumped under the covers.

"C-come in." He trembled inside, remembering that he wasn't really sure of anything, except that his name was Bartholomew Kangaroo. Where was he? How did he get here? Was he in danger? Who was there, opening the door?

First came the rim of a brown hat with an orange flower, and then into the room stepped a little lady, dressed all in brown: brown shoes, brown stockings, and a brown dress. She had long brown hair fastened in a ball at the back of her head, and when she turned, he saw that her eyes were brown, too.

"Hello, my name is Miss Lucy. How are you feeling?"

"Fine, thank you, but...."

"Never mind the questions. Just have some breakfast, and I'll do the talking."

There were hot buttered muffins, red raspberry jam, steaming porridge, and foamy rich chocolate, all in lovely silver dishes set on a white cloth. The thing that pleased Bartholomew most was one red flower sitting on the tray Miss Lucy put across his lap after he sat up.

"Mr. Bear found you last night. You were unconscious in the middle of the road, so he picked you up and brought you home. Dr. Raccoon came as soon as we called him. He dressed the cut on your head and said that you were in no danger, but that the blow must have been quite severe. You must rest for several days. He will come to see you again sometime today."

The Kangaroo was having a difficult time. There had been so many things to think about. He hadn't realized just how hungry he was, until Miss Lucy brought him breakfast. Now thoroughly amazed he was trying to eat, and listen, and understand, all at one time. When he wanted to nod his head to show he understood, and to take a drink of chocolate at the same time, there was also a matter of precedence to decide.

All this was almost too much for him. Though the breakfast was delicious, and though he was interested in what this nice lady was saying, still.... Miss Lucy was saying: "We are all happy to have you here...," when she noticed he was fast asleep. "Poor fellow, he is a bit weak, I'm afraid, but sleep will help." She removed the tray and pulled the covers gently up around his shoulders.

Miss Lucy had picked up the tray and marched (she usually did in the mornings) as far as the door, when she remembered a look in the kangaroo's

eye when he first saw the tray. So she went back to the small table and left the vase with the lovely red flower where he could see it as soon as he awakened.

Bartholomew never forgot that day. It was so full of happenings. It was a wonder they all found time to occur. When he awoke again there was his friend the red flower, and that made him feel all light inside. Soon afterward the doctor came into the room and Bartholomew liked him right away. The doctor was gentle. He looked wise, and he had eyes that were so kind that Bartholomew forgot to be at all afraid. The doctor put a cold metal disc on Bartholomew's chest. It tickled. He looked deep in Bartholomew's eyes, and tapped Bartholomew's knees. He put some lavender pills in a bottle, and wrote some instructions for taking.

"Now young man, see you rest, eat well, lie quietly, and you will be fit as a fiddle before we know it."

"Oh, yes, sir," said Bartholomew, his eyes solemn and big.

As Dr. Raccoon was leaving, Miss Lucy came into the room, and smiled at Bartholomew before she asked the physician; "How is he?"

"Even better than I expected. Quiet pursuits, sleep and delicacies will have him completely mended in no time."

"Fine, fine, and is he allowed company?" Miss Lucy wanted to know.

The doctor didn't seem to look at Bartholomew at all, but he noted a small fidget that Bartholomew couldn't stop, so he said; "Well, perhaps my good friend Mr. Bear may be allowed in for a while, but no one else."

Bartholomew relaxed. If this Mr. Bear was a good friend of the doctor's, surely there was no need to feel afraid, was there?

The doctor said goodbye and went off with Miss Lucy, so Bartholomew went back to looking around him at the room.

The windows with the padded seat and the table with the yellow flowers were on his right, as was a tall chest of many drawers beside the bed. At the foot of the bed and across the room was the singing fireplace, with a rocking chair on one side and a stool on the other. On both sides of the fireplace, from the floor to the ceiling, were shelves of books, books of every kind, except where a tiny desk had been placed among them, near the window.

"Oh, what a nice room! What a wonderful place to stay." He wondered if it would be all right if he called it *his* room. He said softly: "My room. Please come in." Like magic it was, for he was certain he hadn't said a word, nor had he heard a knock. Had he? Still, the door opened, and there was a Real Personage. Bartholomew was sure he was a Personage because he stood-with-a-manner, and because he was portly.

"Thought I'd stop by and see how you were getting on," said the Personage. "My name is Mr. Bear."

"How do you do, Mr. Bear, I'm Bartholomew Kangaroo, thank you."

The eyes of Mr. Bear looked intently into Bartholomew's own, and Bartholomew was somehow proud he could look right back. Mr. Bear seemed satisfied after a blink or two, for he said: "Ah, well, nasty contusion you have there, but the doctor assures us you will be mended soon. Just obey his orders, and you'll soon be about. Afraid I may have disturbed you this morning. I was playing a game of croquet with myself, as usual, when I realized you were ill up here, and needing your sleep."

"Oh, no, sir, I was awake."

"Fine, fine. Good game, indoor croquet. Perhaps you would like to play a round when you're able?"

"Oh, yes, thank you, sir. I should like that very much."

Mr. Bear smiled, looked to a grand gold watch from his vest pocket for advice on the time, and cleared his throat. "Well, I must go...meeting of the council in the village...see you again soon."

"The Council," thought Bartholomew," Mr. Bear must be very important. His suit is so fine, and everything about him is exactly so, but he seemed friendly, and not frightening at all."

Kangaroo spent the next few days eating and resting. He tried to read, but slept instead, and after three days realized that he was well.

Miss Lucy came to see him several times every day. Once she brought a baked madlar tart, smothered in cream; another time a slice of spiced prune cake and a glass of cold milk. For dinner one day Bartholomew had nut fillet, sauteed artichokes, wild rice, heart-of-palm salad, and bulber berries with lime ice for dessert.

Now Bartholomew's mind was fuzzy. He couldn't remember a thing except his name, but he was certain that these things were surely delicacies, just as the doctor had prescribed.

Whenever she brought something to him, Miss Lucy always talked in a brisky fashion while he was eating, so Bartholomew gradually learned about "the family": all the people who lived in this large house.

"The bulber berries were grown by Rabbit. He is not much of a conversationalist," said Miss Lucy, "but he is so nice, never out of temper. He spends most of his time out in the garden during the day, and reads "The Agriculturist" in the evenings while he plays records."

Kangaroo thought to himself that Rabbit sounded nice indeed, and he looked forward to meeting him soon.

She told him about Mr. Bear: how he liked to play at croquet, or lawn bowling, how he was a member of the town council, and of the board of education, and was the local magistrate. "Everyone respects him," she said, "and when he goes walking, someone is always running out to say hello, or to ask for help or advice. There is also Chester Dog. He is the really extraordinary member of the household. He writes, you know."

Bartholomew realized that Miss Lucy was proud of Chester Dog, and he was prepared to hear more about this gifted author, but Miss Lucy saw the grocery boy coming up the driveway, so she hurried downstairs.

When the doctor examined Bartholomew that afternoon, he gave him permission to sit up in a chair, and said, "You can take your meals downstairs tomorrow, provided you don't walk around so much as to tire yourself."

"Oh, I shall be careful," said Bartholomew, and he was so excited at the prospect that he hopped up and down in bed.

Chapter 2

Introductions

Rabbit was alone, as he generally preferred to be, wondering about the new carrots. They were a special type. He had sent all the way to Burbank Downs for the seed. They had been planted for five days now, and Rabbit was eager to see the tiny green feathers appear through the black ground he had prepared so carefully.

"Carrots—what more could anyone want?" thought Rabbit. He was concerned with his carrots, each one of prize winning quality. He had more varieties than any other member of the Carrot Society. Nowhere in the civilized world, he confidently thought, could anyone pull from a garden, or a field, a more richly coloured, juice filled, sweet tasting, crunchy carrot.

"Ah................" The long sigh which Rabbit let slowly float upon the fresh air of the garden bespoke contentment such as few have ever known. Rabbit knew that everything was fine in his life. His people were nice people; his garden was all he wanted it to be; and there was time for everything he wanted to do.

"Such a fine life," mused Rabbit. The sun warmed his back to a glow. Above, in the taller trees, small zephyr puffs were whishing back and forth.

Several butterflies were floating, like confetti forever on the wind. Well, it was almost time to brush up for lunch. That poor fellow who had the accident was coming down to lunch for the first time. Rabbit pulled three thistles from a bed of marjoram and patted a bit more dirt around some weak young chervil plants he had transplanted only yesterday. "Te, ta, de, de, da, de," hummed Rabbit, and "Pat, pat, pat, ti pat," went his deft little hands, as he fixed one, two, three, four plants.

A sudden booming caused him to straighten up with an astonished look. "The Bittern Bell! It's time for lunch. Oh, well..." He washed his hands under the hose, smoothed his hair and brushed the dirt from his trouser knees. Straightening his shirt, he walked quickly toward the house, for he certainly didn't want to be late. That wouldn't be proper at all. Rabbit was glad when he saw that everyone was just arriving.

Chester Dog was seated, and Mr. Bear was gazing out of the window. Here came Miss Lucy and the new fellow.

"He's a strange one," Rabbit was thinking, when Miss Lucy introduced Bartholomew.

"How do you do, Mr. Rabbit," Bartholomew said. "I'm pleased to know you, and thank you for all the wonderful delicacies you sent while I was ill, especially the bulber berries."

Rabbit felt fine about being remembered before everyone in this way, and decided that this was a good fellow after all, and not at all strange. He felt shy, though, and shifted his feet about, but then he noticed that Bartholomew was smiling at him. That smile fixed everything between them so they were tight friends, without even realizing it had happened.

Lunch was very pleasant for Rabbit. Miss Lucy and Mr. Bear did most of the talking. Rabbit and Mr. Dog didn't say much, and Rabbit guessed that Bartholomew was the quiet kind also, or perhaps he was just unused to all of them.

"Oh, Rabbit", Mr. Bear said; "I ordered the imported Irish moss you wanted. Mr. Pruggle will deliver it as soon as it arrives from the city."

"Mr. Bear, you are most kind..."

"'Twas the very simplest matter, nothing at all. You see, I wanted to see Mr. Pruggle anyway. He's one of the aldermen, and I wanted to inquire what he could do about the large hole at Botta Lane and Layard Road. Almost broke my neck last evening on my way home from the meeting of the Heraldic Society."

Rabbit wondered how Mr. Bear could stand so many meetings. He supposed someone had to look after all those sorts of things, and Mr. Bear seemed to like it, so everything worked out. Rabbit knew, on the other hand, that Mr. Bear didn't like gardens at all, except for looking purposes. The thought of getting dirt "about my person," as Mr. Bear put it, made him positively ill, and upset him for days.

Now Rabbit was hardly ever more content or happy than when he was working in the middle of his plants. Rabbit especially liked edible plants: fruits, herbs, vegetables and first, of course, carrots. He had nothing against flowers and liked to look at them, but he only had so much time, and none to spare for flower-growing. The house could use a good flower gardener.

"My goodness, are you going to sit there all day? How do you expect Meg to clear away?"

Rabbit started. He was the only one left at the table, and Miss Lucy was looking down at him from beside his chair at the head of the long board.

"Bless you, wool-gathering again," and she walked toward the kitchen door.

Rabbit went quickly out to his garden on the far side of the property, away from the house. The paths, as he trotted along in his usual quick way of walking, were glinting in the sun. It was quite warm for so early in the spring, and Rabbit wondered for the hundredth time that day if those new carrots were sprouted yet.

"I'll just have another look." He sighed. "No, not yet." Still he bent his small back into a deeper bow, and peered more intently. Suddenly he leapt in the air, turned around, and singing, "Tra tra la la la," ran all the way back to the house. He ran into the library where he snatched a magnifying glass from the shelf and ran all the long way back to the garden. On the ground again with the magnifying glass in his hand, a pleased smile sudden-ly twitched Rabbit's nose. There it was! A tiny dot of green had broken through the earth. His new carrots had sprouted, the special "Golden Treasures."

Notwithstanding the fact that Mr. Bear didn't like to work in the dirt as did Rabbit, he didn't abhor exercise, or exertion, if it wasn't senselessly strenuous. He decided to take a walk, since the weather was so favorable.

"Early spring this year, I think," he thought to himself. "Hmmmm, yes, yes." Bear walked along, turning over the brown oaken leaves with his ebony cane. Soon he found what he expected, a tiny purple flower, bloom-ing a smile.

"Hmmm, hmmm, so nice," thought Mr. Bear, and smiled, too. He walked on down the lane under the oaks, looking over the hills that were starting to be touched with green, fading to blue in the distances.

"Snmf, snmf." Mr. Bear always made snmflly sounds when he started to think deeply, or when he had a special problem. He was thinking now about Kangaroo, and what a pity it was the poor fellow had lost his memory, though it didn't seem to bother him much.

"He has recovered and seems to like it here well enough. He certainly is pleasant," said Mr. Bear to himself. "I like him. I shall ask him to stay." Having made this decision, Mr. Bear made his shoulders very square, pulled himself inches taller, and sauntered on down the lane, admiring the country hills, and the trees, and putting his cane down in a distinct manner every two and one-half steps. How good it was to be a bear!

Chester Dog was not happy at all. He had been trying to write the middle stanza of a poem, but somehow the words would not get together properly. Chester was in his room upstairs, which was just like the one Bartholomew had: fireplace, windows, and long window seat. One thing was different, however, and that was the books. Chester didn't buy shoes, or hats, or clothes. He bought books. Instead of spending his money on candy, or magazines, or picture puzzles, he spent it on books. Mostly he liked books that were older, books bent at the corners and worn at the seams; books whose pages had lost their shine, some yellow-tinted with age, and showing drawings of extraordinary interest. Though Miss Lucy tried to provide shelves enough for Chester's books, there were always many extra ones; they were piled against the wall, and on top of the desk. They were piled under the bed, with only the titles showing, or by the comfortable chair in a stack, ready for reading.

Chester was lying with his face down, on the window seat. His royal-blue composition book was on the floor, and though he thought and thought, and rolled his eyes this way and that, still the right words would not come. He couldn't write today. Maybe he should go and see his Tree.

When Chester felt sad, or when he was discouraged he always went to his Tree. When he sat there and heard the birds in the tall branches, he always felt better. Sometimes the wind whirled the Tree around as though it were dancing, or whispered in the needles. In the winter snowflakes sifted down and made the branches look as though they were decorated in white icing. Chester was such a retiring sort that the way he felt when he sat under his Tree, hidden from everyone, suited him exactly.

Chester sat up, put one leg on the floor, then the other. "Goodness me, why won't this poem help me a little? Maybe the publishers are correct, and I'll never be able to write. I'll never become a good author." Chester became forlorn, but thin notes from a tiny violin made him look up. It was the signal that he was wanted downstairs. When anyone in the hall downstairs turned a small handle three times around, the small wooden man over Chester's door raised his arms and played a short tune. Chester started downstairs, but before he reached the stairway Miss Lucy could be heard:

"Hurry, hurry, you slow one, it's a telegram! Indigo Jones just brought it over from the village."

There was Mr. Indigo Jones in his uniform, with his hat on the back of his head, his bold eyes fixed on Chester as he gave him the telegram-yellow envelope. "Hurry up, let's see what's in it boy," he said in his rough voice.

Chester had never received a telegram in his whole life, nor had he ever seen anyone else get one, so he didn't know what to do. He just wanted to be back in his room worrying about his latest poem. He wanted to forget all about this telegram. It was such an upsetting thing. Why didn't Mr. Indigo Jones go away, now that he had delivered it? Why did Miss Lucy and he both just stand there? Didn't they know it embarrassed a fellow? Chester didn't know what to do, so he just stood also, with brown eyes wide open, bewildered. Miss Lucy finally opened the envelope and read the message. "You've won this year's International Olive Leaf Award for poetry. You'll be famous."

"Oh," said Chester. "Oh," and he turned around and went out the door into the yard. He went across to the far corner where his Tree was. He had a lot to think about. It was all confusing to the shy dog, and he wasn't sure he liked it. He wondered what it would mean. Now that he considered, he didn't have the slightest idea what the Olive Leaf Award was, what it might mean to other people, or what he was supposed to do. He hoped he would be left alone as usual. He would have to ask Mr. Bear for advice. Mr. Bear knew all about these things. Yes, there was the solution: Mr. Bear would help him, for Mr. Bear was like that, always ready with comfort or aid. Chester felt better and as he listened, the sound of birdsong and wind made him forget his anxiety. Away up there was the blue sky. Through the needles of his Tree he could see bits of sugar-spun clouds going for a sail, and there were sheep-clouds and flower-clouds ... and a dragon, and...and... and Chester was sound asleep.

Chapter 3
The Kitchen, the Gardens

Miss Lucy loved occasions of all kinds, and she thought this was surely an occasion of the first order. What an honor for all of them. As this *was* an occasion, she was going to make a cake. Miss Lucy loved making cakes, but only a little more, perhaps, than Mr. Bear and Rabbit and Dog liked to eat them. She went out to the kitchen and looked at the shelf where she kept her cookbooks. Miss Lucy had more cookbooks than anyone in the entire county. She kept them on shelves near the big round oak table in the corner of the kitchen. She selected four books, and started leafing through first one and then another, trying to see something that seemed special and also would please Chester Dog. She looked only at recipes made with chocolate or peach, Chester's favorite flavors. She looked in the book called: *"Extraordinary Recipes of the Century"* and in *"The Favorite Cakes of the Knights,"* but it wasn't until she looked in her rarest cookbook that she found the cake recipe that she thought would be exactly right. This book was called *"A Touch of Magic,"* and had been kept carefully by the members of Miss Lucy's family for many, many years. The book contained recipes to be made for special events only. If anyone tried to use the recipes otherwise, the undertaking was doomed to failure, failure in the usual ways: a bowl upset, a custard filling burnt, or some essential ingredient forgotten—but failure, in any event.

Miss Lucy felt justified, however, in consulting this book now, and she chose to make the crushed peach custard meringue cake. Out came the grand blue mixing bowl, the silver sifter, spoons, and beaters. Out came four cake pans, a sauce pan, measuring cups, and a jar of sun-dried peaches. She was ready to begin. Before she actually started the mixing, Miss Lucy went to the door leading into the dining room, where there was a shining bell, affixed to a brass arm that was fastened to the wall. She grasped the silken cord that hung from the bell and pulled it smartly, three times. This was a well understood signal throughout the household. Anyone interested could come to the kitchen and watch, or talk, or taste the sample cake, or lick the remainders left in any of the bowls or saucepans. Someone was sure to appear before the cake was ready for the oven. All the family liked the kitchen, for it was always bright and fragrant. There was a nice feeling about this kitchen that everyone could sense—it wanted people to be comfortable, to eat, and to talk as only friends can. In the summer time, the coolest breezes came through the door that opened from the springhouse; and when the winds were abroad with snow swirls, the fireplace sported a glowing red heart that warmed and murmured at once.

Miss Lucy was beating egg yolks when she heard footsteps. But, instead of coming in a marching way, as footsteps usually do, these came a little...hesitated...and stopped.

"Sab, sab, sab," the spoon said, as Miss Lucy stirred the cake batter, "sab, sab, sab."

Miss Lucy looked up, wondering to herself, "Who is that? I don't recognize that step at all." She didn't see anyone. She was just going to look back to her beating, when three moving spots in the doorway caught her attention. She was so intrigued by the strange things, one white, and the other two brown and leathery, that she dropped the spoon and ran toward the door. There, looking shyly around the corner, so only his nose and the tops of his two ears could be seen, was Bartholomew. A very embarrassed Bartholomew, to be sure, when he saw he had so amazed Miss Lucy.

"Oh...I...I was just coming to see why the bell was ringing. It sounded as though it was coming from here."

"So it was, come on into the kitchen, Bartholomew. That was the Invitation Bell, to let everyone know I am baking a cake if they care to come to talk or taste. I should have told you about it, now you are a member of our family."

Bartholomew's eyes were larger and blacker that instant than ever, and perhaps a bit moist, too. "Am I really a member of the family?" he asked, afraid to say it so boldly.

"Well, you are if you want to be, and we'd like you to stay if you would. We should be very happy to have you."

Bartholomew looked at her as though he wasn't sure if he should laugh or cry. Two tears formed, one in each of his eyes, while his ears folded together over his head, as they did whenever he was excited. My! He was the happiest animal at the end of the green lane at that moment. A family of his own!

Miss Lucy seemed to know how full of feelings Bartholomew was at that moment, for she went right back to her mixing. "Sab, sab, sab," went the spoon. Soon she had the small sample cake ready for putting into the oven.

Bartholomew was sitting watching her all this time, and thinking that this kitchen was indeed a very magnificent place. The special smell of the small boxes of spices was very entrancing, so he went over to read the names: bay leaves, basil (sweet), cardamom, cinnamon, comino, caraway, coriander, marjoram, mustard, mace, sage, savory, saxifrage, saffron, sorrel, and so many more. All the while he was looking at the spices and the sauces and the extracts and the flavorings, Bartholomew heard the little silvery noise that running water makes, and though he looked around he couldn't see any water. So he decided that the noise came from beyond that open door. There, in the middle of the next room, was a spring. It bubbled up into a gray stone basin that was about three feet high. The cold water swirled merrily around, flowed along three stone channels for a few feet, then sank into a hole, and disappeared. Bartholomew noticed there were crocks of butter sitting in the water, pots of cheese and large jars of milk, while fruit of all sorts was piled in wicker woven baskets, placed so as to catch the fine drops of spray. Upon shelves around the rock walls of the room were all manner of things that are better when cool: vegetables, eggs, nuts and such. Within easy reach was a big pitcher of pink lemonade.

"Bartholomew, will you bring me the green bottle of milk?" asked Miss Lucy.

Bartholomew picked it up from the icy water, and carried it into the kitchen. "Here you are, Miss Lucy," he said, proud he had been asked to help. Then he noticed that everyone was there in the room: Mr. Bear, Rabbit, and Chester Dog, who looked as though he had just waked, which of course he had.

Miss Lucy took the sample cake from the oven, and it was large enough for everyone to have a slice. She poured glasses of creamy milk and handed around the steaming cake. The vote was unanimous: "Delicious!" So Miss Lucy put the four pans containing the rest of the batter into the oven.

Mr. Bear told them how he had finally introduced his "Bill for the Abolishment of Traps" to the council that afternoon. "It is going to be a fight, I'm afraid," he said. "Those favoring the legislation, and the opposition, are so nearly equal, we need something to aid us, and to swing the balance our way."

"It's a disgrace," fumed Miss Lucy, "there are only a few in the village who are so barbarous, anyway."

"Perhaps," said Rabbit, "if we all consider this matter, and discuss it from time to time, one of us will think of something in time before the bill is voted upon."

"That's a fine idea," boomed Mr. Bear, and they all agreed.

Chapter 4
A Tour of the Grounds

When Bartholomew was entirely well, Rabbit asked him if he would like to see the gardens. Bartholomew's ears flew together on top of his head, but all he said was, in the most restrained fashion, though he was very excited, "Why yes, Mr. Rabbit, if you can spare the time." He had wanted to see the gardens, and especially the flowers, ever since he saw the blossoms in his room the day he awakened in the house.

Bartholomew and Mr. Rabbit walked out through the kitchen, so Mr. Rabbit showed him the vegetable garden first.

"This is for Miss Lucy, at her request. We grow everything here except turnips, which upset Chester." They passed to a smooth green lawn. Rabbit explained that this was Mr. Bear's croquet and bowling lawn, and showed him the small pool with a bottom of blue crystal. Then, they crossed the drive and looked at the goldfish swimming in a large pond. On the other side of the circular drive, they came to another velvety lawn.

"This is called the Lantern Lawn, where the annual lantern contest is held. It is great fun, and all the people of the countryside come. You'll like it, Bartholomew."

They walked on through a copse of silver birch, through the tingling, shaking leaves. Bartholomew saw the small meadow in the woods where the wild strawberries were to be found, and the blackberry thicket nearby.

The fruit orchard was next. There were trees of cherries, peaches, plums, apricots, pears, and apples. All the fruit was tiny and green this early in the spring, but it was a beautiful place to be. Chickadees and tomtits jumped around the branches. A bluebird was building a nest, and underneath, rose-veined windflowers were coming into blossom. As the two walked along the paths, birds dipped in their flight to brush Rabbit's hat, or chatter a few liquid notes in his ear, or even to rest a moment on his shoulder.

Bartholomew's eyes got bigger and bigger from seeing all the beautiful things, and he was so pleased by everything that his ears simply stayed tight together, right over his head.

Finally, with pardonable pride, Rabbit took Bartholomew to see his very special section of the garden. "These beds, Bartholomew, are carrots." There was a carrot bed in every shape imaginable. There were long beds, short beds, square beds and round. "Some of these carrots are planted in sand," Rabbit explained, "some have been planted in shell, some in moss, and still others in a mixture." Rabbit went on to show Bartholomew giant carrots with feathery leaves three feet tall, others with medium blunt leaves, and dwarf ones, thin as slender threads. Rabbit even pulled a carrot for him. "This one is called *Saccrinus Candyuus*," he said, washing the golden cone, and presenting it.

"Yes, indeed, Mr. Rabbit, so very sweet, quite tender, too. Most enjoyable."

After they inspected the plantings of herbs, pinched the lemon verbena and exclaimed over the rare nutmeg tree, they walked along a different path back in the direction of the house. They went through a gate in a thick high hedge, and there the path led through a sort of wilderness. Here were roses, overgrown, and vines all intertangled. A few poor stringy flowers tried to climb over the thick growth of matted weeds toward the sunshine, but with little success. Bulbs pushed through the unworked ground, but came up

with twisted leaves. Grass crawled over the once white pebble walks.

"Goodness, what is this place?" asked Bartholomew.

"This is the terrace garden. It is just outside the windows of the music room and the library."

"I never noticed anything outside of that window but a hedge."

"That's right. The shrubs and trees are so overgrown you can't see a bit of this. We left the shrubs untrimmed like that on purpose, so this mess wouldn't be seen from the house."

"Why isn't this garden cared for, like all the rest?" asked the bewildered Bartholomew.

"Well, we haven't been able to find anyone who wanted to take care of it," said Rabbit. "All of us have our special jobs, and there is no other gardener available anywhere."

"Would it be a big job?" inquired Bartholomew.

"Oh, goodness, yes. I wouldn't want the job myself," said Rabbit. "But now it is time for lunch."

Chapter 5
Birds and a Plan for Music

Chester usually stayed up later than anyone else in the house; he read, or he wrote, or sometimes he just sat, and stared into the fire and thought. Because he was up until later at night, he slept later in the morning, but on this particular morning he was awakened abysmally early, just after the sun came up, by a great deal of chirruping. There was such an amount of noise, Chester pattered to the window, and looked outside, but there was nothing unusual out in the garden, so he dressed and went downstairs. The noise was louder here.

"I believe I hear Bear's voice."

When he opened the door, he met a scene of confusion. Kangaroo was busy buttering twelve pans of muffins that were still steaming from the oven heat. Rabbit was filling saucers with honeyed blackberries, and Miss Lucy was stirring a cauldron of chocolate on the stove. Still, over all the activity, and under it, and all around it, was the chirruping and the twittering. What did it mean?

Chester went over to Miss Lucy and shouted: "What's happened?"

Miss Lucy looked around, "Oh, good morning, Chester, dear, I'm afraid they have waked you. I'm so sorry, but it couldn't be helped. Perhaps you can have a nap later, when they are gone."

"They?" said Chester. "Who are they? Why can't it be helped? What is all the noise? What happened?"

"The birds lost their way," replied Miss Lucy. "They were in the Spring Migration, when a terrible storm on the higher levels blew them miles from the route they usually follow. After flying over unfamiliar country all night, the leader saw our place. He settled his people in the orchard and in the wood while he came here to inquire about directions. I found out the poor things hadn't had a bite since yesterday morning, so we are fixing a little breakfast. Bear sent the leader to bring them to the side garden. After they have eaten and rested, Mr. Bear will help them find the correct route. There, now, the chocolate is ready. Is everything else finished?"

"This is the last muffin to butter," said Bartholomew."

"Yes, the berries are all served," answered Rabbit.

Everyone worked quickly, Chester and Mr. Bear included. Soon the hungry little visitors were having a pleasant breakfast under the trees. However, when Chester, who had been in the kitchen, carried out his first tray of buttered muffins, he almost dropped it in his surprise. Never had he seen so many birds. The trees were covered with them and seemed alive with their flutterings. The grass was not to be seen, there were so many of the tiny feathered beings, and looking at them all, Chester became a little dizzy, for the solid earth seemed to move. The movements of the birds made it seem to swell, and shift, and sink, and then flow in different directions. They were all cheerful, though, and smiling, and many of them wished Chester a heartfelt good morning.

When all had been served, Miss Lucy hurried inside, where, with Bartholomew's help, she spread platters with chopped nuts and millet as a special treat for the visitors. She knew how dearly birds like this combination and how it keeps them well.

Mr. Bear went into the library and came back almost staggering under a load of books and maps. He took them to show the leaders of the migration so that they could find the way to their summer home. He sent Chester back for the globe and he also used the almanac, *Burrough's Guide to Good Roads*, and *Hints to Pilots*. Mr. Bear was thorough in being helpful, for that was how he was. The birds were soon on their way, refreshed, rested, and confident of their route. The members of the family stood at the kitchen door to wave goodbye. The birds circled once in parting, and were soon just a dark smudge along the horizon.

After the birds were gone everyone went inside the kitchen and sat down, content to rest awhile after all the excitement. Meg, the girl from the village who helped out, arrived, fortunately, and made steaming cups of tea for each. Rabbit revived first and observed, "Too bad all our birds are not as nice as those fellows seemed to be."

"Why Rabbit, what do you mean?" said Mr. Bear. "I'm sure our particular birds are equally as nice. That was an unkind thing to say, not a bit like you. Would you explain?"

"I'm sure," interrupted Chester, "there must be a reason for you to speak so strongly, eh, Rabbit?"

Rabbit was a bit confused at first by the reaction to his words. "Goodness, I didn't mean to reflect a bit on our own lovely bird families. I was just thinking I hadn't seen those rascally cowbirds for at least a week, and that is a bad sign. You have probably never even seen these knaves. They live in a thicket beyond the back wall, and never come up as far as the house. They're a thieving lot, and too lazy to even build their own nests. I wonder what they are up to this time. Every time I don't see them for awhile I know they are plotting something. They love nothing better than to steal my carrots. I keep a sharp watch, and with the help of the electric catcher that is attached to my carrots, I have nothing to fear, I guess."

"I see I owe you an apology, Rabbit," said Mr. Bear, "and more so, for I've seen two of that very family of cowbirds, the Johnsons, talking to Farmer Grump." Bear stopped talking, arose, and looked around the table. "Grump is heading the group that favors the use of traps. There isn't a week goes by that some poor innocent isn't hurt at his place."

"Perhaps he's hiring the Johnsons to do some of his underhanded work," said Miss Lucy. "You had better keep a watch on him."

"Let us know what is going on, will you Mr. Bear?" said Rabbit, as he got up to leave the table. "Now I must go out to my garden. The patch of new ones needs a little water." Rabbit nodded to everyone and went out the back door.

Bartholomew began to fidget as soon as Rabbit stood up, and now he said, "Is there anything I can do, Miss Lucy?"

"Why, no, Bartholomew, but I thank you, anyway. Why don't you get out into the sunshine?"

Bartholomew smiled and his ears popped up, but he hastily smoothed them down. "That will be nice, I'll go out right now." He hopped, almost skipping, so quickly that Miss Lucy was amazed.

Outside, Bartholomew looked around for a sign of Rabbit. The garden was large and there were many paths leading in every direction; there were hedges so tall Bartholomew couldn't see over them; shrubs and trees he couldn't see through. Nevertheless Bartholomew found the corner where Rabbit's particular garden was located. There he was, in his red shirt, carefully watering his new prize carrots. Bartholomew didn't speak. He sat, screened by a hedge, and peered through, watching everything Rabbit did. He noticed the tools Rabbit used, and how he used them. He saw how Rabbit dug, and removed the weeds and grass from the soil, and prepared a plot for planting. Bartholomew watched as Rabbit took tiny plants from a box where they were growing tightly packed together, and saw him replant them in the prepared soil about 12 inches apart. Bartholomew watched all morning. Then, as soon as the Bittern Bell sounded for luncheon, he hurried away, for he didn't want Rabbit to find him.

After a delicious meal of toasted asparagus and cheese, with puffy potatoes, red crisp radishes, stewed corn, cabbage cooked with cream and an apple surprise for dessert, Bartholomew went into the library.

The library was the nicest place, exactly right for reading. There were thousands of books in the room, covering all the walls, all the way up to the ceiling. There were books with bindings of many colors, deep toned and shining, jewel gleams from reflected light. A big table for writing stood near the windows that opened onto the terrace. There were chairs of all sorts, both hard and soft, and there was light enough to make reading easy.

He needed a certain book. Bartholomew looked for half an hour, taking first one book from the shelf, and then another, but he was still not satisfied, and the search continued. Finally, about three o'clock in the afternoon, when poor Bartholomew was going to admit defeat, and his ears were hanging limply down on either side of his face, he found what he wanted. He sat right down and started to read *For the Beginning Gardener.* Then he read *Care of Roses, Bulbs And How They Grow* and *Soils.*

When it was time for dinner he went to his room to dress, carrying an armful of other books, including *Spring Pruning* and the conservative *Derbyshire Planting List.*

At dinner, Miss Lucy asked, "Did you have an enjoyable time today, Bartholomew? You look so well tonight. You must have profited from the time you spent in the open air?"

"Goodness, yes, young man," said Mr. Bear. "There is no doubt that you are improved by your outing. Take my advice and spend a lot of time out-of-doors. There is nothing so helpful for the constitution, unless it's walking, which is educational as well, of course."

Bartholomew smiled, for he had a secret plan. "A most interesting and enjoyable morning, certainly, and I feel so well," he said, "I think I shall spend all day outside tomorrow, if you all think it is a good idea."

"You surely weren't near my end of the garden, or I should have seen you," said Rabbit.

"Oh," said Bartholomew. "I was just strolling around."

Chester asked Mr. Bear, "If you pass the stationer's will you please order seven reams of foolscap. I find I'm almost out of paper."

"Why certainly, I'd be glad to," said the helpful Mr. Bear.

"You know," said Miss Lucy, "we haven't had a concert since Bartholomew became a member of the family. Wouldn't it be a pleasant treat for us to have one after dinner sometime soon?"

"Why not tomorrow?" asked Rabbit.

"Well, that's a wonderful idea. Shall I invite Godwin Stork? You know he enjoys music," said Mr. Bear.

"Oh, yes, do. I'll attend to the refreshments," Miss Lucy added.

"Rabbit and I will select the program," said Chester.

"My printing is rather good," said Bartholomew, hesitantly. "Would you like me to make a copy of the program for everyone?" There were warm cries of acceptance. "I'll fix the chairs," said Mr. Bear.

Bartholomew was glad to return to his room. He was heavy-footed from so much excitement. But he read for quite some time and learned many things before he turned out his light and went to sleep. He dreamed of trimming rose bushes to the accompaniment of great orchestral music.

Chapter 6
The Terrace Garden

Bartholomew was so eager to do certain things that were part of his plan, that he was the first awake the next morning. He got up, dressed and walked softly past Chester's door, and Mr. Bear's door and downstairs with not even a squeak to tell of his going. The house was so still and strange that Bartholomew just stood for a moment in the hallway, holding himself quiet. He didn't even breathe, and he heard all the odd noises a house makes in the early morning times: snaps, creakings, and a general preparation for the day. Bartholomew went into the games room, opened the outside door, and stepped onto the terrace. He wanted to be sure the wild garden couldn't be seen from any of the windows of the house. It couldn't. The hedge that grew at the foot of the terrace was so thickly overgrown that it was a high wall of green, impossible to see through. Bartholomew looked at the upstairs windows, but he couldn't tell exactly what could be seen from up there. He decided he would investigate more fully later.

Bartholomew walked along the hedge back toward the kitchen, looking for the gate that he and Rabbit used the day he first saw the Wild Garden. "Oh, yes, there it is!" Bartholomew Kangaroo squeezed through. He was back in the wonderful garden. At least, thought Bartholomew, it could be wonderful with some pruning and some spading, and allied things. As he wandered along the paths his heart shook a little. Bartholomew wondered if it were possible for someone who had never been a gardener to become one. This was his plan: to reclaim the Wild Garden, to make it beautiful with flowers, bright with color, and full of sweet fragrances. He wanted it to be a well cared-for garden, where there was always something blooming, and he wanted to accomplish it all in secret. He wanted no one in the family to know what he was about until it was all finished.

Bartholomew looked at the tangled masses of vines and trees, and was discouraged, but not for long. As he walked on exploring, he came to a center circle, from which paths led outward in four directions. As he looked closely, he saw in the very middle of the circle a fountain, almost hidden by thickly matted jasmine. Bartholomew sighed. "What a lovely garden this must have been. But no time for mooning about; time for doing things." He would manage it all, somehow. There were only two problems really worrying him: seeds and tools. Where could he possibly get enough tools? He was fairly certain Rabbit would notice any tools that were missing, if only for a few hours, for he used them every day. Bartholomew had no way of getting things from the village and keeping his secret, so what was he to do? He was so intent upon his problem that he didn't notice how much time had passed since he came into the garden. Now, suddenly, he realized how late it was. He knew that if he was not to be discovered downstairs and so endanger his plan for secrecy, he must hurry. He faced around, darted up the path toward the house, squeezed back through the hedge, slipped inside the games room, and scooted up the stairs. Whooow, what an out-of-breath Kangaroo! He sat on the window seat in his room and stared down at the tree tops in the orchard while he caught his breath. After a while he went to his desk and found pencils, a ruler, and paper. He drew an outline of the area enclosed in the Wild Garden, and then placed within the lines the shapes of the overgrown flower plots. Next he opened one of the books on gardening to a chart, and with a big sheet of paper, he began to work. For his garden there had to be annuals, which just bloom once, and then must be regrown from seed, and perennials, which continue to grow from the same roots year after year. Bartholomew had to remember to plan the flower beds so that the tall flowers would be at the back or inside, with flowers of lower heights coming down to the outside like steps. He had to remember what colors look best together, which flowers prefer shade, and which sunshine; and when each flower bloomed. Bartholomew's head was beginning to hurt; there were so many things to fit together. He was so glad when the Bittern Bell sounded to announce breakfast that he bounced downstairs in the hoppiest way, and right into the kitchen. "Good morning, Miss Lucy," Bartholomew said and he smiled. "How are you, Mr. Bear, Mr. Rabbit?"

"Fine, fine, my boy," said Mr. Bear, "But what has made you so chipper? Did you run around the house, or something?"

"No...oh, no," said Bartholomew with a guilty look, for he didn't realize Mr. Bear was just jesting.

"Lovely sunshine out today," continued Mr. Bear, "I believe I shall walk over to Fartowne today and see the vicar, Mr. Weatheree. We haven't had a game of draughts in months."

"That would be lovely," said Miss Lucy, "I will fix you a lunch, if you'd like."

"Thank you, Miss Lucy, that is most kind. I could ask for nothing better than one of your most excellent snacks. That alone is reason enough for a jaunt."

"Oh, Bartholomew, if we give you the program for tonight's concert at lunch, will that be time enough for you to letter them?" inquired Rabbit.

"Oh, yes, indeed, it will not take long at all," Bartholomew assured him.

Rabbit spoke again. "Mr. Bear, as you'll be going by Mr. Stork's house anyway, would you mind stopping to invite him for tonight?"

"Was just going to suggest it," said Mr. Bear.

Breakfast had never been better. There were hot biscuits, a hot vanilla drink, orange balls, and pease porridge with thick yellow cream. The kitchen had never seemed more pleasant, either, with sunlight making gay bands of yellow on the white curtains, and settling in a circle around the blue bowl of dancing daffodils on the round oaken table.

As soon as everyone had gone from the kitchen, and Meg had cleared away the dishes, Miss Lucy took her dessert and cookie cook books from the shelf, so she could decide what would be a proper refreshment for after the concert. Bartholomew went up to his room, and struggled with names like Ageratum, Campanula, and Dianthus, puzzled what to do with Clematis, Geum, Portulaca, and Helianthus, wondered if Primula would go properly with Delphinium. Poor Bartholomew, he was having such a difficult time. He decided he would go downstairs again, to try to find some implements for working in the garden. First he looked all around the kitchen garden. He found one very small triangle hoe, but that was all, so he went around to the front of the house, to the bowling green, to the gold fish pond, to the lantern lawn, but he had no success. He looked throughout the orchard, and then approached the Wild Garden from the far side. He had never tried to reach it this way, but sure enough he found a gate. He managed to push it open far enough to squeeze through. Just being here made Bartholomew happy. All the hard knots in his mind disappeared, and a quietness seemed to fill the corners of his being until everything seemed good, and no task impossible. He knew he would manage his gardening without tools, if need be. As Bartholomew walked toward the back of the garden a little helping song came to him:

> The day is new, the grass is green,
> The finest day I've ever seen;
> And as I walk or hop along,
> I like to sing a happy song.
> Dum da dee Dum da dee Dee dum...

He sang as he walked along, looking around the garden. Scuff sciff sciff, his feet went right along the gravel as happy feet do until all of a sudden, Bartholomew stubbed his toe and fell. When Bartholomew looked, he noticed he was lying on a large square of wood. It was shaped like a door, and had a large ring affixed in the middle.

Bartholomew brushed the gravel from the surface of the wood with a

twig, then he grasped the ring and pulled. Nothing happened. He pulled again and nothing happened. Finally, he turned and pulled, and the door popped up like a cork. A stairway led to a room some feet below, and there, on the stairs, as though waiting just for him, Bartholomew saw a candlestick and some matches. He struck a match, lit the candle stick and then walked down, down, feeling just a bit edgy.

There was a nice warm smell about the room, and the room was large. There were many shelves all along the walls, and each of them was filled with a great assortment of things. Bartholomew went closer, to see what was on the shelves, and almost swooned with delight! Here was everything a gardener could want! There were innumerable packets of seed. There were bulbs, boxes for planting, shears, rakes and hoes, forks, spades and trowels. There were scissors, knives, sprayers, trimmers, and edgers. Here was the answer to Bartholomew's problem of implements. Now all he needed was time and secrecy to complete his plan. He walked back up the stairs, a very pleased Kangaroo, indeed. He carefully lowered the door and then returned to the house through the orchard.

Lunch was a bustling affair. There was much talk of the concert. Many questions were asked, and advice given. Chester gave Bartholomew the program for the evening's entertainment. After lunch, he went up to his room to do the printing, while Miss Lucy returned to the kitchen and Rabbit worked in his carrot beds.

Chapter 7
The Concert

Mr. Bear put his lunch in his pocket immediately after breakfast, fitted on his cap, took his cane, and walked out through the silver birch lane toward the big meadow. The sun glinted down through the leaves and made bright figures on the brown moist ground. The birds were busy everywhere, building nests, flying through the trees on errands, or twirling in the gay blue sky, and singing. Mr. Bear said hello as he passed, or the birds spoke, but there was no stopping to chat, not this early in the springtime. There was too much to be done by the birds, and Mr. Bear had too far to walk. After Mr. Bear left the woods, he started across the big meadow. The grass was softly green, and there were a few early flowers looking from between the blades. Mr. Bear noticed blue star-shaped phlox, pink periwinkles and one or two primroses.

This was indeed the perfect day for a walk. A happy little wind came along just then, and getting behind Mr. Bear, made him hurry faster than he really cared to go. Still, he chuckled, and whistled a military air for cadence; that's how good he was feeling.

On the far side of the meadow was Mr. Stork's house. Built many years ago, the stone had weathered to a deep red, and it sat in its garden with the comfortable look of a lady in a rocking chair. Mr. Bear walked quickly up the path, stopping only once, just long enough to admire a trailing vine that had been added to the already beautiful garden since his last visit. Mr. Bear rang the ship's bell on the front door. Soon the door opened, and Mr. Stork peered out through his glasses over his long nose.

"Eh? Who's there? Who is it, I say? Oh, you, my friend, Mr. Bear. This is indeed an unusual day. I am most pleased. Would you do me the honor of joining me for a cup of tea? I would like to have your opinion of a new blend of Darjeeling and Ceylon."

"Why, yes, I would appreciate a cup of tea."

"What brings you to my door so early?" asked Mr. Stork.

"Well, I decided to walk over to see the vicar in Fartowne, as it is such a pleasant day," said Mr. Bear. "Also I was commissioned to deliver an invitation from our family to you. We are going to have a concert this evening and request your company."

"That's splendid, I will certainly come," said Mr. Stork, with one of his special long grins.

"Why not come to dinner?" asked Mr. Bear, "I could stop on my way back, and we can walk together, if you'd care to do that."

"Oh yes, that is a fine idea, so kind of you to ask. I'd be delighted." Mr. Stork poured the tea, and the friends had an interesting talk about the latest happenings in the county. They spoke of how well everything was growing, and of how tasty the tea was, until Mr. Bear decided he had better be getting along. He said goodbye to Mr. Stork and set out. "My, it was good to see old friends," he thought, "and it would be nice to see the vicar, too." Mr. Bear walked, whistling again, and swinging his cane in the jauntiest fashion. In no time at all he had traveled two miles, so he sat on the milepost to rest. After a few minutes he heard rustling rushing sounds coming from the field in back of him as though some small animal were running terribly fast through the grass. Mr. Bear turned around, and certain enough, in a few seconds, out burst a frightened looking chipmunk. "Why, Mrs. Chipmunk, what on earth is all this?"

"Thank heaven, Mr. Bear, it's you!" said Mrs. Chipmunk. "I don't know what we would have done if it hadn't been you...and so close too. I thought I should need to go all the way to Mr. Stork's house for help."

"For help, Mrs. Chipmunk? Why, what has happened, and where is Enoch?"

"It's him, what's wrong! The poor dear is caught fast in a trap in farmer Grump's pasture, and no one to help him."

"Show me where he is, immediately!" said Mr. Bear in a firm, charge-of-things voice, as Mrs. Chipmunk led the way back through the grass. She was feeling less anxious, now that help was assured. Nevertheless Mr. Bear asked her what had happened, to keep her mind occupied as they went.

"Well, we were late with our flour to the mill, so we took the short cut through the pasture. None of us animals use this any more since Farmer Grump bought the place, but we were in such a hurry and thought we could surely see anything dangerous. We were crossing the brook by the rocky place when I lost my balance. Enoch ran to my side and before he caught up to me, I heard the awful snap, and there he was, caught fast."

"My goodness, how horrible! But don't worry, for we will have him loosened and fixed up in no time."

They went down a hill, through a stand of oak and elm trees and a few rods farther was the brook, glistening in the sun. There on the far side was Enoch, one leg caught in the cruel trap. Mr. Bear hastened over, seized a big stick that lay handy, and handed it to Mrs. Chipmunk.

"Now," he said, "when I pull this open, just pop in the stick. That's all there is to it, and Enoch will be all right. Mr. Bear grasped the two iron pieces and slowly, inch by inch, forced the strong toothed bars apart. Mrs. Chipmunk wedged in the piece of wood as soon as she was able, and then Enoch started to move his leg. "Just a moment," said Mr. Bear, "let me do it." Carefully and tenderly he moved the trap away, and returned to examine the injured leg. "A bad bruise, but nothing really serious. See, Mrs. Chipmunk, there was a stone caught in the jaws of the trap, that saved Enoch."

"Thank heavens, and you, Mr. Bear," said Mrs. Chipmunk, "I don't know what we would have done if it hadn't been for you."

"My heartfelt gratitude, for your kind and quick assistance," Enoch added. "I only hope to be able to repay your kindness in some way."

"Can you walk?" asked Mr. Bear.

"Yes, I think so, I suppose the worst thing was the fright," replied Mr. Chipmunk.

"Well, if you are sure you can get home without aid, I will be moving along. Be more careful, now, and warn all the animals again to stay away from Grump's farm. Perhaps those that live there should even move, if they can find any place to go. If only we could prevail against Farmer Grump," said Mr. Bear. "Well, I must be off," and he started walking back toward the road. "There must be some way to convince Farmer Grump that his traps are hurting innocent animals who only improve his land and crops, not harm them. There must be some way, if only we could find it."

Mr. Bear worried, but soon the country loveliness soothed away the worries, the white clouds brushed smooth the fretted parts of his mind, and the smiling flowers called back his own smile. He enjoyed his walk after all, and was soon in Fartowne. "This is certainly a pretty little crowd of houses," thought Mr. Bear, "all gathered in a ring around the circle of the park." The white houses with dark trimmings sat there like ladies at tea, with gay flowers for jewels. The vicar lived on the best side of the circle in a small stone house beside the towered church. Mr. Bear admired the thick growth of ivy on the church walls, and reminded himself not to forget to see the stained glass windows again before he returned home. Having arrived at the door of the vicarage by this time, he pulled the bell rope and waited.

Finally Mrs. Weatheree opened the heavy door. "Why Mr. Bear, what a pleasant surprise. The vicar was just saying last week that you hadn't been to see him in such a long time. He wondered if anything was amiss at the End of the Lane."

"Oh, no, Mrs. Weatheree, everything and everyone is well. But tell me, how is the Vicar? I can see you are your usual self, all smiles."

"Yes, indeed, Mr. Bear, I am fine, as usual, and the Vicar is quite hearty.

He will be so glad to see you, I know."

Mr. Bear left his hat and cane with Mrs. Weatheree and proceeded down a small hall that led to the library, where he knocked softly. A special tap: tap, tap...tap...tap tap...and the door flew open. There was the Vicar, who told him: "I've been worried about you. Can you stay long? How is everyone at home? Is there any news? How did you get here? Have you had lunch?" The Vicar shook his hand and patted him on the back and settled him into a chair, and did all this in no time at all, he moved so quickly and spoke so rapidly.

"Hold fast, hold fast," said Mr. Bear with a smile at his impetuous friend. "Go slowly or I shall never be able to catch you. Now, let me see—Oh, yes. Everyone is fine, and all send their regards, even Kangaroo, whom you don't know yet. His arrival is the principal news. I walked over, it was such a pleasing day, and I have not had lunch, though I brought it with me." "You did? Splendid!" said the Vicar, for he expected some nice surprise such as Miss Lucy usually put in the lunches she made.

Mrs. Weatheree brought in two appetizing trays just then, and the gentlemen dined on creamy potato soup, a salad of wood lettuce, slices of almond roast, and green garden beans. When Mr. Bear opened the lunch Miss Lucy had prepared, they found buttered fruit bread sandwiches, the Vicar's favorite. Miss Lucy always did this; she fixed a lunch for Mr. Bear, knowing he would open it after he arrived at the vicarage, so she invariably fixed what the Vicar would like also.

The friends talked for quite some time. Mr. Bear told the Vicar how he had found Bartholomew lying insensible in the roadway, how ill he had been, what a nice member of the family he was, and how they all liked him. Mr. Bear told how worried he was over the traps on Farmer Grump's farm, and of the problems of finding new homes for all those that lived there. The Vicar was interested to hear about the lost migrating birds, and thought Mr. Bear had handled the affair very well.

"By the way," said the Vicar, "how is Mr. Stork?"

"He is well. I stopped at his house for a chat just this morning."

"I would like to see him," returned the Vicar. "I haven't had a talk with him in ages."

"Why not come to our house tonight, then, for he is to be there. We are going to have a concert. Why don't you and Mrs. Weatheree come home with me?"

"Well, that's a grand suggestion. I'd be happy to go along and we'll see about Mrs. Weatheree right now." The Vicar rang the bell, and when Mrs. Weatheree appeared, he questioned her, and found her not only agreeable, but excited at the prospect of the proposed visit. She went off right away, to make herself ready for the trip.

Meanwhile the two friends walked over to the church so the Vicar could play a Bach fugue for Mr. Bear. Mr. Bear sat in the dusky light of the church, admiring the luminious beauty of the stained glass windows, and listened to the powerful music. When the two returned to the library, Mrs. Weatheree was still not downstairs, so Mr. Bear and the Vicar played checkers, another of their favorite games. Finally, Mrs. Weatheree appeared with her hat, gloves, and coat, so the two friends finished their game, with the final score of three for Mr. Bear and only two for the Vicar.

They all had an enjoyable walk, crossing the meadows where the flowers grew thickest, and then following the course of the brook almost to Mr. Stork's door.

Back at the End of the Lane everyone had been busy all afternoon. Miss Lucy had been doing something secret, a surprise, for she had definitely *not* rung the bell, yet such fragrant baking smells floated up the stairs to Bartholomew, and into the music room to Chester and Rabbit, that they were all hungry well before dinner. After she had the special treat prepared, Miss Lucy left Meg to finish dinner and disappeared into her room.

Bartholomew had spent the afternoon in lettering the programs, and such an artistic accomplishment they were. He decorated each cover with a bouquet of spring flowers, drawn in colored inks.

Rabbit cut large bunches of the blue bells and columbine that were blooming in the woods, and he brought some few branches of blooming plum into the house. He and Chester arranged the flowers to advantage, and placed bowls of them on the dining room table, in the hall, in the games room, and of course in several places in the music room. Now everything was in readiness for the night's festivities.

It was so pleasant as Mr. Bear, the Vicar and Mrs. Weatheree were walking through the gentle scenes, talking and enjoying the company, that they soon arrived at Mr. Stork's house, and rang the bell. Mr. Stork was indeed surprised to see his two extra visitors, but pleased. He invited them to "Come in, come in," amid happy greetings. Mr. Bear urged haste, however, and soon the party was on its way across the wide meadow and down Birch Lane.

"My," sighed Mrs. Weatheree, as they approached the House at the End of the Lane, "such a pretty sight." It was surely pleasing to the eyes. The house was of a deep brown-red stone and two stories high. It was built in a U shape. Both wings angled away from the bottom of the U. There were windows across the front; the front door was flanked by lovely cut glass panels, and crowned by an ancient and interesting fanlight. The chimneys stretched many fingers to the sky and shining green-leaved ivy circled the whole. The lawns were close-cropped and verdant, while the trees in the orchard were gleaming with pale pink and white blossoms that sent abroad their fragrance. Snowy white pebbles on the circular drive contrasted with the spring green of the bordering trees. Birds were singing low twilight songs, and the sun had just gone, leaving pale orange streaks in the higher heavens. "Such a pretty sight," repeated Mrs. Weatheree, and everyone was quite in agreement with her.

Soon they were inside the house, and it was "Hello," and "How are you?" "Surprise, surprise!" "Why Vicar!" "Mr. Rabbit, my greetings," "Here, here, let me take your wraps," "So glad you could come to dinner," "Vicar, I should like you to meet Bartholomew Kangaroo," "I just asked them to come along, I'll go find some chairs," "I'll go see about dinner." The whole group was talking at once in the excitement, and it all made an interesting din.

Dinner was very delicious, though there was such friendliness, no one remembered exactly what was served; only that it was one of the best dinners they had ever eaten. After dinner Mr. Bear led the way into the music room, and there were many exclamations on how attractive the room looked, and what lovely flowers there were. When each person was arranged to his or her liking, Chester gave each a program and started the phonograph. There was quiet, except for the music; music, that casts magic spells and encourages high thoughts; music soft and gliding, or gay and lilting; music strong and deep, marching along; music powerful, stirring to the emotions; music, the enjoyable. Afterwards, everyone sat quietly for a time, gradually coming back to the present from the far places.

"Such a nice concert," said Mrs. Weatheree, "I enjoyed every single note of it."

"I would like to commend the program chairman, whoever that might be, for the excellent selections," murmured the Vicar.

"My sentiments also," said Mr. Bear.

"The artist who designed and executed the programs should also be praised," put in Mr. Stork, in his dignified manner, "I can hang it in my parlor."

"Excellent suggestion," approved Mr. Bear, "and the perfect memento of an exceptionally satisfying evening."

"Here we are," interrupted Miss Lucy, wheeling in a laden cart, "a small refreshment." She handed around plates served with a slice of cake, and a cup of syllabub. The cake, they all agreed, was so nearly perfect as to be a work of genius, for it was a delicately pink-tinted concoction with lime green icing, and it tasted like roses! When asked how she ever obtained such flavor, she confessed she had been gathering droplets of dew from a blooming bush outside the kitchen door.

Mr. Bear and Miss Lucy convinced Mrs. Weatheree and the Vicar that it was much too late for them to try to walk home, and Mr. Stork could not be going home alone, either. They must all stay the night.

As everyone went to bed, it was with particular happiness. It had been such a satisfying day, a day full of exactly the right things.

Chapter 8
Bartholomew's Plan

Breakfast the next morning was pleasant. Soon afterwards the three visitors departed for home. Rabbit went out to inspect his new carrots, Miss Lucy retired to her room to paint while the light was right, and Mr. Bear was off to the village to attend a council meeting. Everyone was busy. Bartholomew made sure of that before he went into "his" part of the garden. He had decided that today he would begin. He had read thoroughly about how to make a garden, and now he decided it was time to get started.

Bartholomew was quite pleased as he sat down to rest, for it seemed to him that quite a lot had been accomplished with one morning's work. As he sat there thinking about what to do next, a discouraging thought came to him. "My goodness," he said to himself, "I know this garden cannot be observed from any of the windows of the house, but how can I be sure of secrecy when there are gates at each end of the paths, where anyone might enter? Oh, gracious, what can I do? However," and his ears stood up, "now I seem to remember Mr. Bear saying that no one ever came through here. If that is true, there is little chance of anyone finding a way in, but perhaps I can fix the gates so they appear stuck." So he was off to look at them. Sure enough, the hedge had grown all around the gate at the back of the garden so that it wouldn't open at all. Bartholomew turned toward the gate nearest Rabbit's carrot garden, and found several long sprays of rosebush growing conveniently near. He twined these around the branches of the hedge that already grew across the gate, making an effective bar to its being opened. However, to be extra sure, Bartholomew wedged sticks under the gate as well. The third gate, that opened into the orchard, had a lock on it, and this he fastened securely. Bartholomew felt better now, for he was sure his secret was safe.

For many, many days, from early morning until time for dinner, Bartholomew worked in the wildwood garden. If anyone asked him where he had been, he would just say he had been walking, or reading in his room, or

some such answer. There was one whole week when he did nothing at all but trim and prune the rose bushes, and he got many a scratch.

The hedge had to be trimmed until it was smooth-sided. This took another week. Bartholomew hadn't realized just how much work it took to make a garden, but he felt it was quite worth the trouble, for ever so slowly the place was becoming lovely. The weeds were all gone. The flower seeds sprouted, grew each day, and the ground was prepared for them to be transplanted. The vines were trained over the trellises which he made with care, and some new vines with different colored flowers were planted.

The bees were the first to discover what beauty Bartholomew was creating, and as the first few fragrant blossoms opened, they came to call, with their golden buzzing. All the watering and spading and tender care Bartholomew put into the garden gave him ample reward. Soon the whole place was almost ready to bloom. Still, the fountain needed to be cleaned, so after that had been done, and the sides scoured briskly with a stiff brush, Bartholomew turned on the water, holding his breath to see if the fountain would work. There was a gurgle, a bubbling of air, three distinct hissing sounds, and then the water shot up. Up, up—into the air, then the silver stream divided, and fell downward in graceful umbrella lines, into the great basin at the bottom. "Oh, goodness!" Bartholomew felt his breath curl into a knot inside his chest. It was such a lovely fountain.

Now that everything was ready, he would need a way to tell the other members of his family, and he finally decided to have a surprise tea the very next afternoon. With that resolution he went inside to the kitchen and conferred with Meg. The two of them planned a menu, consisting of toasted nut-bread and butter sandwiches, tea, milk and some wonderful rolls from the baker in the village. After they had everything settled, four o'clock was chosen for "A Surprise-With-Refreshment" because everyone enjoyed a small snack about then. Bartholomew inquired if it were possible to serve the repast on the terrace, and she said that it certainly was. So then Bartholomew went in search of the family. To each of them he explained, "There is going to be a special tea on the terrace at four o'clock tomorrow.

Would you please be there?"

Miss Lucy said, "Why Bartholomew, how nice, I most certainly will."

"Yes, Bartholomew, of course," said Mr. Rabbit.

Mr. Bear said, "Oh, yes, I will be delighted, but do you mind if Mr. Stork comes? We are having a croquet game tomorrow at one o'clock so he will be here."

"No, of course I won't mind. Bring him, by all means," said Bartholomew, quite pleased. "It will be good to see him again." With Chester's acceptance, Bartholomew considered the matter arranged.

Bartholomew thought the next day was the most important day he had ever had in all his life, for he wondered if the family would approve of what he had done in the garden. He wondered if they would think his choice of color combinations artistic. He had been working on this surprise so long, and the garden had become now so important to him, that he thought he would never last until tomorrow.

Bartholomew lay in his bed, and he was positive he wouldn't be able to sleep at all, but a singing interrupted him, and it was morning. The surprise day had arrived! Now there was still one very important job to be done before anyone came downstairs, so he hurried out to the garden and collected together shears, long wooden stakes, and a few boards. He took these all to the tall thick hedge which screened the Wildwood Garden from the windows on the terrace. He cut the hedge shorter by sections. As he trimmed it low enough to be seen over, he immediately nailed the limbs onto a board, which was later affixed to a stake driven in at the spot over which the limbs had been cut. This made the hedge look whole again, and as though it had never been disturbed. When Bartholomew had trimmed and refixed in place the wide area abutting the terrace, he tied strings to each stake, and tied these to one long string that streched all the way to the edge of the terrace.

At breakfast even Rabbit seemed excited at the prospect of the special tea-party, and asked: "What is this event for?" even though he knew as well as everyone else that it wasn't necessary to have a reason for a party. "Well,"

Mr. Rabbit replied to the looks he received by way of rebuke, "somehow I just felt there was a reason, and I wanted to know what it was." Miss Lucy, too, asked questions, and Mr. Bear made jests, but Bartholomew just smiled wisely, and wouldn't be tricked by Chester, either, into divulging the secret ahead of time.

After luncheon, Bartholomew moved the necessary furniture out upon the terrace, with Chester's help, and then gathered a bouquet of flowers from the secret garden for the table. All was at last in readiness. Meg even had the tea wagon arranged when Bartholomew went to see if everything was in order. Bartholomew put on his newest suit, and after smoothing down his ears and trying to keep them still, he went downstairs again, to the terrace.

It was only 3:30, but everyone appeared almost at once, they were so eager for the party to begin. Miss Lucy looked pretty in a blue gown; Rabbit was shining and brushed; and Chester was wonderfully attired in his best. Mr. Bear, who was generally spruce, had donned a new cravat, and even Mr. Stork boasted a new ribbon on his eyeglasses. Everyone was talking.

Miss Lucy said, "Really, we should come out here more often, the air is so soft and fragrant,"

"Yes," said Rabbit, with a twitch of his nose, "the fragrance is unusually strong. I can't imagine what is blooming."

"Have another plum roll, Mr. Stork," said Mr. Bear, and "Bartholomew, you aren't eating your sandwich. Do you feel all right?"

"So kind of you to plan this tea-party, Mr. Kangaroo. Such a pleasant treat," said Mr. Stork. "By the way, the illustration you so cleverly drew for the concert has been duly framed and it looks very handsome. You are a promising artist, my boy. That is something you should work upon."

"Thank you, sir," said Bartholomew.

"My, my," murmured Chester Dog, "we were lucky the day you came to us, Bartholomew. Tell me, my good friend, where did you get that bouquet of flowers? Such excellent specimens. They show the touch of a master gardener."

"Indeed they do," agreed Rabbit.

"Came from the florist's, I shouldn't wonder," was Mr. Bear's guess. "Extraordinary size!" Bartholomew was all red with pleasure, and he stepped over to the edge of the terrace and picked up the string. He carried it to Miss Lucy. It pulled tight, but he gave her the end easily; it was exactly long enough. Anticipation drew all attention to the string. "Pull it, Miss Lucy, if you will," said Bartholomew.

"Why Bartholomew what is it?" she asked.

"Something I've been doing for some time, and I hope you all like it. Go ahead and pull." Miss Lucy did as he bid her. Slowly, part by part, the hedge, so tall, so thick, and hiding only a tangled wildwood garden, fell. Fell with a crash, and that was a surprise. One gasp followed another, as they all gazed at the new garden. No one spoke. They just sat looking trying to see everything at once. Rainbow arrays of water fell from the fountain and made water pearls and diamonds as they splashed to the pool below. Miss Lucy noticed the blue flowers: larkspur, forget-me-nots, bachelor buttons, and delphinium.

"Oh Bartholomew, so lovely," she said softly.

"Bully," was Mr. Bear's comment, though he looked pleased enough to explode.

Everyone rose from the tables and walked down the stairs except Bartholomew and Chester. Bartholomew looked over at Chester, and saw a tear roll slowly down his cheek, which Chester brushed away. "It is just so beautiful. How thoughtful of you to think of doing this for us, Bartholomew. You are a brick." Chester was a little shamefaced for having said so much, so he patted Bartholomew once on the back, and went down to join the rest. Bartholomew sat there looking, filled with content. He had done a creditable job. The fragrance in the air, the masses of color and the large blossoms all testified to that, and when Bartholomew thought of the pleased faces of his family, and of the pat Chester had given him on the back, he was so happy he thought he must surely burst.

Chapter 9
Alarms and Excursions

For many days Rabbit had been watching his new prize carrots, the Golden Treasures, very intently. In just one week the Conference for County Carrot Growers was to be held, and he well knew that his carrots would win the prize, if nothing in the nature of a catastrophe occurred. The Cowbird Brothers were taunting Rabbit from the fence, where they were sitting in a line, but he ignored them as usual, for he thought they were only bent on harmless mischief. They had been calling raucously all the morning, and this irritated Rabbit, but it wasn't until after luncheon that the real trouble began. Danny Cowbird, after being particularly insulting to Rabbit, disappeared for half an hour and then returned. He talked to the other brothers a few moments, flew over one of the carrot patches and dropped something. Rabbit saw it fall, so he walked over to see what it was. He had to go carefully, so as not to harm any of the tender green tops. Imagine what abject horror Rabbit felt when he discovered that Danny Cowbird had dropped several seed pods of the dangerous Devil's Finger! This was a weed pest which could choke the carrots in a short time if allowed to sprout and grow. This insult was too much for the patience of Rabbit. Those Cowbirds could call him names or make rude remarks if they would, for he was too busy thinking of other things even to hear. However, when these vandals put deadly weed seeds in his garden, that was something to fight about. He jumped up, and looked around, but all the Cowbirds had disappeared. He picked up all the seeds most carefully, but immediately the Cowbirds returned, each one carrying something! More of that devilish weed! Rabbit was aghast. Everything in the garden would be ruined if he didn't stop them, but what could one do against so many? He had an idea that might help, but he must hurry. He ran to the faucet and turned on the water to full force. He grasped the nozzle tightly, and turned it toward the diving rascals. The water whooshed out in a strong stream, and the amazed Cowbirds did somersaults in the air backwards, and flew away from the pelting water. Luckily, in the excitement, the Cowbirds dropped the seeds beyond the wall. As he flew away, Danny Cowbird shrieked: "Ha, you fooled us that time, but we'll fix you. Wait and see. Come on, the rest of you, let's go get more weed seed." They flew wheeling away.

Rabbit ran for the house. When he got near he started to call, "Alarm, alarm! Everyone is needed, a crisis is at hand!"

Miss Lucy heard from upstairs, and ran out with a purple smudge on her nose, for she had been painting. Mr. Bear harrumphed out of the library where he had been writing a letter to the *Times*, and Chester popped from the music room. Bartholomew had been trimming the hedge outside the kitchen windows, so he reached Rabbit first. "What has happened? Where?" he asked.

But Rabbit hadn't any breath left to answer, and when he was finally able to do so, all the members of the family had arrived. He told them briefly of what had happened and what the Cowbirds had threatened.

"An outright violation of property rights," gruffed Mr. Bear emphatically. "We shall go to law about this."

"That's an excellent idea," said Miss Lucy, "for Monday, but what are we to do now to save Rabbit's garden?"

"The main thing we need," Rabbit began, "is something to repel them.

The water is good for one person to handle, but do the rest of you have any ideas?"

"I have just the thing," said Miss Lucy. "I'll get what I need and meet you in the garden."

"Why, of course," Mr. Bear broke in. "Why didn't I think of that sooner?" And he trotted off in the direction of the orchard.

Chester darted into the house. Bartholomew, who had been looking worried, went in the direction of his garden.

The Cowbirds looked over the wall from the thick wild bush, but there was no one in sight, not even Mr. Rabbit. This should have warned them, but they were so malicious, so intent on the harm they were doing, that not one of them gave the matter any attention. The leader, Danny, gave the twenty or so members of his group last instructions: "That Rabbit's garden will be fixed for good," he said in his raspy voice. "Be sure every seed falls in the garden."

"We will. We'll fix that stuck-up Rabbit."

"Let's do it, then," Danny grinned. "No hurry though, there's no one here. We can even walk about if we want." Then the cowbirds flew in one great flapping, rustling mass over the wall. No sooner were they over the line, than everything happened at once!

Years later, the story was told by elderly cowbirds to fledgelings as an illustration of the dangers of wickedness. But in talking about the catastrophe later, the participants disagreed on exactly what happened.

A great screeching, yelling, whooping, gruffling and moaning was the first indication of the things to come. This noise was so strong and loud that it caused a disturbance in the air, currents making it very difficult to fly. A moment after the din came the missiles. "A terrible collection, fearfully mixed with swirling streams of icy water," was the way one cowbird described it. Making a cloud of missiles were Bartholomew's big pebbles, Chester's hard paper wads, stiff old muffins thrown by Miss Lucy, green wild thistles from Mr. Rabbit. In addition was the water from the hose wielded by Mr. Bear. The din and the pelting went on and on and on. The Cowbirds were

frightened, overwhelmed, confounded, battered, beaten, and morally destroyed! Completely routed, Danny cried for mercy, and Rabbit agreed to pacify his angry companions if the cowbirds would promise to leave the country with their leader.

"Yes, yes, yes, yes, oh, yes, anything, anything, only stop, stop, make them stop," chattered Danny.

"Ho! Stop!" sang out Rabbit. "The fight is won!" At that the staunch defenders ceased shouting, stopped throwing, and came out from their hiding places beneath the trees, and behind the bushes. The fight was won!

"My, such excitement," said Miss Lucy, "I think I shall just go bake some teacakes, and we will all have a small something to eat."

"Goodness, we'd surely like that," said Bartholomew and Chester together. Then they smiled.

"Hard work, repelling the invaders," said Mr. Bear.

"Well acquitted, my captains," said Mr. Rabbit.

Before dinner, they all went out to the garden again. "All ready to see the special carrots?" began Mr. Rabbit, and he pushed some of the dirt aside so that Miss Lucy could see the bright orange of an extra large carrot.

"My, what an expert you are with carrots," she said. "These are the most important carrots in your whole collection, aren't they?"

"Yes, Miss Lucy," Rabbit was justly proud. "Yes, all my hopes for the prize are in these golden vegetables. I've just missed winning for three years now, but I know these will be awarded the blue ribbon. These six carrots," he pointed, "marked with these sticks, are the ones I shall enter."

"They are splendid! You are surely going to win," said Bartholomew, and Mr. Bear and Chester agreed.

The day had been so exciting that everyone was in bed quite early, and the house darkened. All through the grounds was stillness...on the lawns, in the orchards, under the beech trees, nothing moved...But what was that? There, in the corner of Rabbit's garden? Four figures were digging silently and with great caution. Finally they lifted something, and put it in a box that was standing ready. Each grasped a corner, and at a signal, flew upwards, over the wall and into the wild thicket. Those Cowbirds, those lying Cowbirds!

Rabbit awoke and wondered what had distrubed his sleep. He was uneasy for some reason, so he put on his slippers and a robe and went out to the garden with a flashlight. He saw the hole immediately, for he went to see the prize carrots first...and they were gone! They had been stolen!

Chapter 10
Victory and a Picnic

There was nothing so black as poor Rabbit's hopes at that moment. His plans were ruined, and there was nothing that could help him. A small breeze tugged with the fringe of the belt he wore with his robe; it danced a stately measure with the green tops of the remaining carrots and spiraled to the tip branches of the fir trees. Rabbit sat on the wheel of an overturned wheelbarrow and put his chin in the cup of his hand. He felt calmer...there were other carrots...but no, none would win the coveted prize but *those* six carrots. He would get them back! He made himself a vow. "Not another carrot to eat until I have recovered my prize ones." With that resolution, Rabbit felt better, and decided that he should scan the ground carefully. There might be something he could learn that would help him discover where the thieves had gone. He twitched his nose, adjusted his whiskers, and turned on his flashlight. "Hmmm," there seemed to be four of them, and what was this rectangular hole? "Could they have dug the carrots up with the earth surrounding them?" wondered Rabbit hopefully, for if they were still in soil they would not wilt, at any rate. "Yes, here's the space, and there's the hole!" said Rabbit, inspecting the ground about the cavity. Now, for the first time, Rabbit thought that some of his plans were to be salvaged. If the carrots had been just pulled out of the ground in the ordinary way, the best he could do was to get them back and capture the robbers. If, however, a box of dirt had been taken, with the carrots in the center, then all might be well. The carrots would continue to grow, and would be in excellent condition for the convention. Rabbit skipped on his way back to the house. He was in a hurry, for there were things to prepare, and he must be ready to depart immediately after breakfast. He decided the Cowbirds would not go far until daylight. Perhaps they might even wait until later. They were a lazy bunch, so he hoped he could catch up with them.

Rabbit dressed in sturdy clothing, put on heavy boots, and then tossed things about in his closet, looking for his knapsack. When he finally found it, he started putting in some of the things he would need. There was a bottle of water, compass, first aid materials, a stout length of rope, a jackknife, small hatchet, 3 chocolate bars, an extra handkerchief, and then the straps to be buckled.

Someone knocked on the door. When Rabbit opened it, there was Miss Lucy. "Well, Miss Lucy, what are you doing abroad so early in the morning?"

"Heard you stirring earlier, and saw your light when I awoke just now. Is something wrong?"

"Yes, the Cowbirds sneaked over the wall in the night, and stole the six prize carrots."

"Oh, Rabbit, not your special ones, for showing at the convention!"

"Yes, Miss Lucy, but I'm going to have them back. You'll see, I shall have them back in time for the judging."

"But how will you do that?" Miss Lucy wanted to know.

"I shall simply hunt for them until I find them, of course," replied Rabbit, steadfastly.

"You are so brave, Mr. Rabbit, but Mr. Bear had better go along. In dealing with those wretched Cowbirds, one can't be too careful. Breakfast will be in a few minutes. I will hurry it along."

Rabbit put on his jacket, and in the pocket put a reading glass, several packets of gumdrops, a folding cup, a ball of string, an alarm whistle, dark glasses, a telescope, the latest edition of Dimlow's *County Road and Lane Guide,* and a piece of red crayon. There was just no telling what would be needed for a venture of this kind.

Downstairs, Miss Lucy had a hot breakfast ready, as she had promised. Rabbit sat down at the table in the kitchen and started to eat. Mr. Bear came precipitately in a few seconds later.

"What's this, what's this? What was stolen?"

"Why, I told you," said Miss Lucy.

"I know, but you were so excited I could hardly understand what you were talking about, and then you dashed away," said Mr. Bear. "Your carrots are gone, Mr. Rabbit?"

"Yes, but I am going to get them back. It is most fortunate, too, that the plants were seemingly dug up in a bunch, with plenty of earth around them. Now, Mr. Bear, don't feel you must go along. This is really my trouble."

"Nonsense, my boy. I must go, and I shall enjoy it anyway. Excellent excuse for an outing. Besides, we must have none of this lawlessness in the community. So glad the prize carrots were stolen so carefully. We at least have a chance, and you'll win yet."

"Thank you Mr. Bear," said Rabbit. "Are you nearly ready to leave?"

"Here you are," said Miss Lucy, giving each a lunch to put in his pocket.

A very sleepy Bartholomew came around the door, into the kitchen. "What's happening? Why are you two dressed like that? Where are you going?" he asked, as his ears stood up, and his eyes popped awake. When the two travelers had explained, Bartholomew said, "Wait for me!" So he ran upstairs, and Miss Lucy started to fix him a lunch, also. Chester Dog arrived in the kitchen just then, and the story was re-told. Chester was indignant that the Cowbirds should break their word, and rob Rabbit into the bargain, and he demanded to be taken along.

Finally he and Bartholomew came downstairs with all the paraphernalia they thought necessary. Miss Lucy gave them lunches, and the searchers filed out the kitchen door. Rabbit was in the lead, followed by Mr. Bear, Bartholomew, and Chester last in line, carrying his camera. He hoped to get some photographs of the culprits, if nothing else. Into the yard, down the paths, across the carrot plots, and straight to the wall, Rabbit led the way. When he was at the bottom of the wall, he and Mr. Bear put up a ladder and climbed up. Chester and Bartholomew watched them going up...up...up...and it was so far Bartholomew felt quite small, all of a sudden. Then he looked over at Chester, and knew Chester felt exactly the same way. As they stood there, looking at one another, a strange and good thing happened. Suddenly each of them knew, again, he had found a friend, and the tall ladder was easy to climb. They smiled at each other and started up.

When everyone had reached the top of the wall, they pulled up the ladder and let it down into the darkness of the underbrush that grew on the wild side. "Remember," said Mr. Bear, "we must be careful here."

"Yes, indeed," agreed Mr. Rabbit. "We must stay close together. No telling what we may find in this wilderness. From what the bird families tell me, the Cowbirds live on a rocky ledge in a canyon quite some miles away. We may hope to catch them, however, for they won't be able to travel quickly with something heavy to carry."

"We had better hide this ladder, before we go on," suggested Bartholomew, so it was hastily concealed in some thick bushes. Mr. Bear led the way through the trees, but they had gone only a little way before Chester called a halt. He had found a lost feather belonging to a Cowbird, and not only that, but many footprints, and marks of a box having rested on the very spot!

This cheered everyone, and away they went, walking rapidly, and each one looking keenly about, to discover more traces of the thieves. The wild places were very beautiful and quiet. The trees were tall, with heavy foliage that kept out most of the sun, which had now risen, but the soft blue green light of the forest was pleasant, and there was a rustling hush over everything. "My, Chester, isn't it strange?" whispered Bartholomew. "Can it be those awful Cowbirds really live here?"

"Oh, no," replied Mr. Bear, "they just fly through here because it's shorter."

"We must go through the woods and around the lake, for those rascals live on the other side," explained Rabbit.

Soon another set of footprints was found, and afterwards another. Finally Mr. Bear decided he had better climb a tall tree to see if he could locate the Cowbirds. Chester and Bartholomew were glad of the chance to rest. Three hours of walking was more than they were accustomed to doing, and they were tired. Rabbit, however, walked cautiously ahead, to see what he could discover and he soon came back to report.

"The trees are thinning out. I think we are nearing the lake."

"Ho, there," called Mr. Bear from above, as he slid down the tree. "We are almost up with them. My spy glass was a real aid. They are only a mile away. We will catch them sooner than I expected. Not only that, they are tiring. They rested twice while I watched."

"Have they any idea we are following them?" Mr. Rabbit wanted to know.

"No, I don't think so," replied Mr. Bear. "Not one of them looked around. I guess they don't expect us for a few hours yet."

Chester spoke, "It was certainly fortunate you awoke when you did, Mr. Rabbit."

"By the way, how are we going to capture them?" Bartholomew inquired. "We must have a plan ready."

"Well," Rabbit replied, "there are four of them and four of us, but we certainly don't want any real violence. I have a net. We could each take a corner, and throw it over them. That way there would be no opportunity for them to hurt the carrots."

"Yes, good, fine," everyone agreed.

After another half hour's walking, Mr. Bear again mounted a tree, and came hastily, but softly down.

"They have just stopped to rest about a hundred rods away. We can catch them easily if we hurry."

"Here's the net," said Rabbit, who was tremendously worried about his carrots."

"Let's go!"

"How are we going to do this?" asked Bartholomew, who was not at all certain of his fitness for catching thieves.

"Well," Mr. Bear snuffled as he thought, "they are just under a rock on the lake shore. If we stay directly back of that rock, we are screened from their observation as we advance. We can also drop the net to good advantage from there, and that is highly desirable."

The friends walked quickly to a point only a few feet away from the rock that Mr. Bear had mentioned.

"Shshhhhhsh, shh," everyone said together. They crept quietly toward the Cowbirds.

There were the Cowbirds, cackling at the top of their voices! Danny was telling coarse jokes, to which the rest responded with raucous laughter, and all were boasting how they had gotten revenge on the snobbish Rabbit. Danny was telling them what he would do with his share of the money when they won the prize at the Carrot Convention. "Why, I just think I'll move to one of those fashionable cities beside the ocean where the better people spend the summer, and. . ." Just then there was a whish, and a gray mesh fell upon the ruffish birds.

Later, no Cowbird agreed on exactly what had happened. The four friends had gotten close to the rock, each had taken an end of the net, and they silently spread out. They crept nearer, and nearer, until they were just above the culprits. A silent signal had been arranged beforehand, to be given by Mr. Bear. Mr. Bear gave the signal and the net flew out and over the Cowbirds. However, one end of the net caught upon an outcrop of stone, and didn't go all the way to the ground. Mr. Bear and Chester ran to the right from the rock, and Rabbit and Bartholomew ran to the left, trying to reach the Cowbirds and tie them up. The Cowbirds were screaming, flapping their wings wildly and trying to escape. Danny, however, remained somewhat cool and noticed the one open side, so he was quickly under the net and away in a flip, followed closely by his henchmen, all of them almost grey with the fear of being captured. Mr. Bear and the rest jumped unsuccessfully after the escaping birds. Rabbit's first concern was for the prize carrots. His loud wail brought everyone running. "They're gone, the carrots are gone, they're not here, oh gracious!"

"Stand fast!" It was the calm deep voice of Mr. Bear. "Rabbit, we shall find the carrots. I know they are here, for I saw them. Chester, Bartholomew, we must all endeavor to find the carrots at once. You two look over there, Mr. Rabbit can search here, and I shall look on the far side."

Bartholomew walked over to Rabbit, who had been strong for so long, and said to him: "It won't be but a moment, we will find them quickly, I'm sure."

"Thank you, Bartholomew," said Rabbit. "I guess I was just discouraged for a moment. Let us look."

"Here, here," came the rolling voice of Mr. Bear. Rabbit rushed over to a crevice in the rocks and, sure enough, there were the prize carrots. They looked as undisturbed as though they had never been moved from the pleasant garden at the big house.

Rabbit let out all his anxiety in a sigh, and sat down on a rock, and smiled. His Golden Treasures, his prize carrots, were safe. There was much laughter, congratulations, smiles, and then Chester proposed, "Why don't we have a picnic? There over close to the lake is a table rock, under that shady tree. We all have lunches."

"Good, good, said Bartholomew, and Mr. Bear and Mr. Rabbit agreed, so the company had Miss Lucy's delicious lunch, and drank from the lake. After eating and a short rest, Mr. Bear suggested it was time to return. This time they enjoyed their walk through the woody wild places, delighting in the thick ferns growing intermingled with fair flowers and stately trees.

After the long walk home, the explanations, eating dinner, and all the general excitement, it was no wonder that the whole family was asleep early that evening.

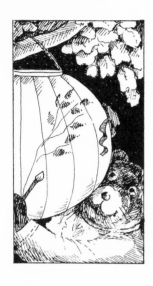

Chapter 11
The Lantern Festival

When Mr. Rabbit left for the Carrot Convention, Miss Lucy gave him a long list. "Don't forget to place the order for all these things, for we will need them in only two weeks."

"Is the Lantern Festival that soon?" asked Chester.

"Yes, it is," returned Miss Lucy, "and there is much preparation necessary before then. We must all set about seeing that everything is ready."

"List? Preparation? For what?" asked Bartholomew Kangaroo, timidly.

"Well," they all began at once, then each one stopped, waiting for the others to go on.

Finally Mr. Bear, who was always an excellent spokesman, explained: "Every year, when the season is exactly right, we have the Lantern Festival here. We invite everyone. There are games, and contests, and refreshments. The most important prize, always something special, is given to whomever makes the most beautiful lantern."

"How are the lanterns made?" inquired Bartholomew, his eyes shining and his ears lifting with excitement. This sounded like fun!

Miss Lucy continued, "That is my special charge. I collect all kinds of paper and cloth throughout the year, as well as foils, tissues, and different materials; anything, in fact, that can be made into lanterns. For the contest, which is open to all, we set up many long tables, and provide scissors, needles, thread, pots of glue, paints, crayons and gummed tapes. Three hours are allowed for the making. Then the judges confer, and award the prize."

"And that's not all, Bartholomew. The very best is as yet untold," Chester broke into the conversation. "After the awarding, refreshments are served and then at dusk, the lanterns are hung in the trees and are lighted. Bartholomew, it is something you must see!"

"Is there anything I can do to help?" Bartholomew wanted to know. "What about a general review of all the gardens and lawns, and getting them all trimmed and weeded? I could get Meg's brothers to help."

"Mr. Kangaroo," said Mr. Bear, bowing, "you are, indeed, indispensible. Miss Lucy and I were wondering who was going to do that very essential task just last evening. With Mr. Rabbit away, we were duly perplexed, as you can imagine. We thank you for your thoughtfulness, and accept your offer."

Meanwhile Mr. Rabbit was on his way to the convention, holding the precious carrots on his lap so nothing could possibly happen to them. The carrots had a specially built container this time, with a "moisture-saving temperature control." Rabbit was proud when he saw the admiring glances of the other travelers on the train, who noticed the vigorous green leaves through the glass sides of the case. At the convention, Mr. Rabbit was indeed acclaimed the foremost carrot grower for his six extraordinary specimens. In addition to the prize monies, a sumptuous banquet was given to honor him. During the dinner Rabbit was requested to read a monograph he had just written, entitled, "The Development and Cultivation of New Hybrids," which gained him the acclaim of scholars. Rabbit had achieved distinction in good measure, and he was feted, and noticed wherever he went in the convention city. Those at home were pleased to have their own Mr. Rabbit so recognized. They read every detail of the happenings as they were reported in the papers each day. When he arrived back at the station, Mr. Bear met him. Miss Lucy baked him one of the Special Cakes (Orange Cream-fondant Five Layer Cake). He was kept talking until every detail of his trip had been told.

During Mr. Rabbit's absence, preparations for the Lantern Festival were progressing nicely. Mr. Bear had been making arrangements with the caterers in the village about refreshments and a menu had been selected: syllabub, ginger punch, hot chocolate, tea, lemonade, and strawberry soda for drinking. For those who were hungry there were assorted sandwiches of sixteen different kinds, and desserts, also. Mr. Bear had an affinity for desserts, and he planned for red raspberries with whipped cream, sponge-peach pudding, apple dumplings, chocolate torte, ice cream in six flavors, pineapple and lemon sherbets, fresh coconut cake, vanilla pecan pie, cranberry tarts, and cavalier buns. There were to be vegetables, almond roasts, onion stews, six salads and cream soups.

Miss Lucy had been busy in the cellar, where the paper was stored, sorting colored papers in piles, and separating the piles, so much to a box. She had been busy in the attic, also, making a collection of silks and cottons, velvets, batistes and shantungs. Chester had collected bottles of glue, pairs of scissors, thread, wire and pots of paste.

"Will we ever get all these flower beds weeded and the hedges trimmed, and the grass cut in time?" Bartholomew wondered. He was as busy as anyone, out in the gardens. Meg's seven little brothers were swarming over everything with shears and hoes, mowers and rakes. The large trees were all given a trimming and so were the hedges. The flower beds were cleaned of weeds, dead leaves were removed from the bushes and fresh potted plants set along the paths. The lawns were clipped close, so they looked velvet-smooth, and all the edges trimmed. Walkways were raked clean, and everything was washed with sprays of water. Soon there was not a stray bit of dust anywhere. Each blade of grass shone, and the gardens all seemed waiting happily for the big party. An air of expectancy hovered over everything, as last duties were finished, shoes polished, ribbons pressed and suits brushed. All over the county that night, as last preparations were being completed, children talked of the lanterns they would make on the morrow, and the parents spoke of the same thing. Eyes sparkled, and snatches of song drifted out of lighted windows into the darkness. This was the best festivity of the summer, a dream party, where everything was exactly right.

Bartholomew was so excited his ears had been standing straight up for three whole days, and no amount of concentration would get them down. As soon as the sun arose the next morning, he was wide awake and eager for the day to begin. At breakfast the family talked about the party, of course, and Chester submitted for approval a list of the music to be played.

Somehow the morning was over, lunch had been hastily eaten, every hair was combed, and it was time for the guests to arrive. They came traipsing along, and singing in the merriest way. Greetings ran through the air like tiny bells, and there was a hum of cheery conversation everywhere. At two o'clock the Bittern Bell was rung. That was the signal for the games to begin on the bowling green to the left of the house. Such games, such fun! Running; jumping; singing and skipping rope. There were games for the children, for the parents, and for the grandparents. Some were for the swift to win, some were for the strong, and there were games for the thoughful to win, also. Those who didn't enter a contest cheered on the others; and those who didn't compete one time, did so the next. Prizes were given to the winners; delightful things of the sort that made even the losers glad.

Finally the Bittern Bell sounded again as a signal for the lantern making. Mr. Bear explained the rules completely, as he always did so well, and everyone set to work. There was no hurry, for each knew long before what he was going to do. It was just a matter of selecting the materials, and creating the lantern. It was a matter of hoping this one was the grandest one of them all.

Mr. Bear had always begged off making a lantern, saying he was too clumsy for that sort of thing, but this year he was going to try. The lanterns were such lovely things, and Mr. Bear admired them so much. He chose a piece of pale yellow silk which he stretched very carefully over a wire frame he had made. Mr. Bear never worked harder, nor had such satisfaction from anything as he had from making this lantern. Smooth and shining were the sides after he had sewn them on, and then he was ready for the rest of the decoration. Ink, and black paint, and a tall stalk of bamboo with a few leaves on one side of the silk. That was all. Mr. Bear sat back, relaxed, and looked at what he had made. He was satisfied, for he knew it was beautiful, and it didn't matter what the judging decided.

The time allowed for making the lanterns ended just as Mr. Bear put his lantern in the line. As he walked about, waiting for the judges to announce the winner, one of the caterers came to ask Mr. Bear a few questions, which he answered. He talked longer than he knew, however, for in the middle of his last sentence he was interrupted by a great gusty cheering. He walked toward the large circle made by the curving driveway, and where the award was to be made.

The award this year was still a secret, though everyone had heard it was truly exceptional. The Art Guild was supplying it. Some said the prize had been given to the Art Guild by an old miner who was fabulously rich. The president of the Guild had been heard to say that there was absolutely nothing like it anywhere in the world. Mr. Bear heard loud calls, and they sounded exactly like: "Mr. Bear! Mr. Bear! Mr. Bear!" They were saying his name till it echoed all around him. Someone saw him, and urged him on, faster and faster, until there he was standing in the middle of the circle. He was a bit bewildered, and not quite understanding why he was wanted. Then, suddenly, he understood and his heart was so warm it felt twice as large as usual.

"Mr. Bear, we are delighted to award the first prize, and in the opinion of the judge, this is one of the loveliest lanterns ever made at any festival." Mr. Bear, usually so poised, so familiar with speaking before crowds, couldn't say a word, he was so choked with pleasure.

"Thank you," he stuttered at last, and it was enough. Oh, the cheers! "Hurray; Hurray; Good; Good for Mr. Bear," until the whole place was full of sound. Everyone liked Mr. Bear. "The Prize, The Prize! Let us see the prize!" the crowd began to chant.

"What is it?" Miss Lucy wanted to know. "Hurry, hurry and open it, Mr. Bear. Do hurry or we shall all perish from excitement."

"All right, just hold fast a second, and I shall have the knots untied. Here goes the string." All the watching eyes moved with his fingers as he pulled the string from around the package. "There," said Mr. Bear, "I've loosened the paper. Oh, here's more string and more paper." There was no conversation at all now, as everyone waited. "We finished that paper and string quickly," muttered Mr. Bear, and then he lifted the top from the box. Lying in a bed of dark velvet was the most lustrous, glinting stone anyone had ever seen.

"Oooooooohh," a sigh went round the crowd as they saw the beautiful gem. Mr. Bear took the stone in his hand (where it fit so well it might have been made for this hand alone) and held it aloft to give everyone a better view. The sunbeams were dancing a farewell circle around the gardens, and a few of the gleams happened to touch the wondrous stone. Then, like real magic, tiny perfect faery rainbows darted out in every direction on flecks of shining light. There were audible gasps at this display, and Mr. Bear was almost beside himself with delight and awe.

"A rainbow stone, a real rainbow stone, I am indeed a most fortunate bear," he thought to himself.

"Dinner will now be served," announced Miss Lucy, "on the bowling green."

"The tables are already set," mentioned one adventurous chipmunk who had already gone exploring. "Let's hurry. There are all sorts of good things for everybody."

Mr. Rabbit assisted in helping people to find the particular delicacies they liked: "Mrs Brampton, do try this almond roast." or "Will you have a cup of tea?" and so on.

Bartholomew, too, was helping. "There are seats this way." "Could I get you a glass of punch?"

House at the End of the Lane

Miss Lucy was seemingly everywhere at once, saying to Mr. Stork, "I'll just cut you a piece of this cake," and to one of the Robin children down at the other side of the large table, "Would you like another sandwich?" Next, she was back talking to Mr. Stork again, "We haven't seen you at all lately. Why don't you come over next week for bowling and dinner?"

There was much laughter, enjoyment and happiness as dinner was eaten. Then the visitors strolled about looking at the gardens, admiring the flowers, exclaiming at the abundance of fruits or wondering at the smoothness of the lawns. Finally, in the darkening sky of twilight, the lamps, now hung in the trees, were lighted and the music began. In the cool silence of the blue dusk, the notes of the flute rippled, and the violins and cellos sang, accompanied by the harpsichord. The golden light of the lanterns encircled loveliness within their beams almost too wonderful to believe. It was a night of enchantment, and this was the last hour of a perfect day.

Before the music had quite ended people began to slip softly away. There were no goodnights, or thank yous; the spell was too strong. No loud sounds disturbed the quieter melodies. Soon only the moon was left, smiling down on the empty garden, where the lanterns soon flickered and went out, one after another.

Chapter 12
Two Triumphs

Several days were necessary for the house to return to its quiet ways after all the excitement, but finally the place was as restful as ever. Butterflies sailed in and out of the gardens, birds threw gay earfuls of music into the calm air, and bees hummed a deep summer song.

"My gracious," said Miss Lucy one morning as she walked out in Bartholomew's garden. "Bartholomew, this is the most beautiful garden I have ever seen. It is my opinion that your color schemes are simply perfect."

"Oh, thank you, Miss Lucy," replied Bartholomew. "I wasn't sure about my choices, but they seem to have been proper ones."

"Proper ones, indeed. You are much too modest. Would I be in the way if I sat here, by the fountain?"

"Why, no, Miss Lucy," Bartholomew said, with tiny wrinkles on his forehead, as he wondered exactly what Miss Lucy was going to do.

"See?" Miss Lucy had a small folding chair in her hand, and a box under her arm. "My paints. This is such a colorful scene, I must try to paint it. The light is just right, too. Don't you let me disturb you. What are you planting?"

"Oh, I'm only sowing some perennial phlox for next spring. They do better, the *Garden Guide* suggests, if the seeds are in the ground during the winter." Miss Lucy had selected her brush and started to paint, peering out from under the wide brimmed hat that completely hid her face.

"Miss Lucy?"

"Yes, Bartholomew?"

"Has something been bothering Mr. Bear?"

"You are very perceptive to notice. He has seemed somewhat upset. However, he hasn't said anything out of the ordinary to me, except to mention that the Council has some new plans 'for the wider community.' I don't know what that means, and he didn't explain."

"I don't know what it means either," murmured Bartholomew, "but I do wish Mr. Bear felt better. Now the only time he smiles is when he looks at the Rainbow Stone, and then it is really not a very healthy smile. It is hard to remember that he was once the jolliest of people."

"Yes, Bartholomew, he has always had a happy disposition, until about a week ago. Oh, hello, Rabbit."

"Hello, Miss Lucy. I knew you were here. I came to tell you there is a stranger coming up the driveway. Were either of you expecting a visitor?"

"No," said Miss Lucy and Bartholomew, together. Then she continued, "No matter though, for Chester is in the house to answer the door."

"Oh, I didn't know he was at home."

"Thank you anyway, Rabbit."

At the house, Chester Dog was curled in a large leather chair reading a heavy volume on the poets of the Eighteenth Century. He heard the bell ring, but he didn't pay any attention. When the bell rang again in another minute, he decided he had better attend to answering the summons himself. Chester had a pair of glasses with dark rims that he sometimes wore, not because the glasses helped him see better, but because he thought he looked more dignified with them on, and more scholarly. Before he opened the door Chester adjusted the glasses on his nose, adjusted his whole face to dignity, took a deep breath, and turned the handle. On the steps stood a

sturdy man with blue eyes and pale looking hair.

"I would like to see Mr. Chester Dog," he said.

"Won't you come inside?" said Chester, wondering who this was and what anyone on earth could possibly want with him.

"Thank you," said the man, following Chester into the library. After they were seated the man explained: "I am Mr. Thundergaard. Do you remember receiving several letters from me?"

Chester was embarrassed. "I haven't opened any of my mail for several months, so I may find your letters upstairs on my desk . . ."

"Well," Mr. Thundergaard continued, "did you receive notification that you had been selected for The International Olive Leaf Award for Poetry?"

"Yes, I did, and though, quite frankly, I was disturbed at first, after some consideration I was pleased by the honor, and wrote a letter to the committee to that effect."

"Something must have happened to that letter, for I represent the committee, and we received no such letter."

"Oh, dear me," apologized Chester, "I was sure I had mailed that letter. Why, I remember, I put on my jacket, this one, to be exact, and put the letter right in this pocket, so I wouldn't forget to mail it." Chester put his hand in his pocket. His eyebrows went up, then down, and he looked at the floor a moment. He took his hand out of his pocket, and there was the letter! "I guess I didn't mail it after all," was all he could manage to say.

"No matter, Mr. Dog, no matter at all. I have simply come to make the official award for your splendid poetry, and to give you this bronze plaque."

"Hmmmm," said Chester, as he took the shining shield. He was very pleased, but all he said was, "Thank you, this will look fine in my room. Thank you very much. Would you have dinner with us?"

"Thank you. I would like that, Mr. Dog."

Everyone was proud of Chester's fame, and dinner included conversation about the literary world, interesting works in progress and other international affairs. Mr. Thundergaard was persuaded to stay overnight, ate heartily at breakfast and was walked by Chester to the station to catch the ten o'clock train.

Much happened during the golden months of summer. There isn't room to tell it completely, but some things must be mentioned. Miss Lucy won a prize for her cake at the Fair, as well as a blue ribbon for her picture painted in watercolor. It was titled "Bird on a Bough." Both of these things pleased her very much, of course. Mr. Bear and Mr. Stork organized a croquet tournament for the players thereabouts, at which the Vicar and Mr. Stork won all the honors. Chester wrote so much during this time that he used sixteen reams of paper, which is certainly a great deal, so Mr. Bear had a whole load sent out from town, and stored in the attic. This meant Chester was never again left in the middle of the night with a spendid idea, and no paper to write it down.

Mr. Rabbit was busy with his new business, that of seedsman. So many people sent requests to buy seeds of his now famous carrots, that Rabbit started a small business. He was also busy with plans for developing other carrots of his own. Bartholomew was busy in his part of the garden, plant-ing bulbs and seeds as the months passed and the trees dropped their now red dresses.

Mr. Bear was also fully occupied, trying to find new homes for all the small families that lived in Farmer Grump's Brook Strip, but with no suc-cess. He was worried about what was to happen to all his friends when Farmer Grump plowed the land as he said he would do in the fall. Finally, as a last effort, Mr. Bear went to the farmer's house and rang the bell.

"Goodness, gracious me, but there must be something I can say to this man that will make him understand how important it is to the smaller animals not to have their homes destroyed. He should know already, though. He's been told many times these last months."

The door opened, and there was Farmer Grump. "Well," he said, and nothing more.

"I came to talk to you." Mr. Bear was polite.

"Come in then," replied Farmer Grump in a surly tone, as he led the way to the parlor.

Farmer Grump was a square lumpy man with a mouth that turned down at the corners. His voice was raspy, his eyes squinted in a mean way, and he threw in a constant frown, for general unpleasantness. His house was large, white and dirty, for no housekeeper would work for him. Though his farm was the biggest in the county, his crops never grew with abundance, as they did for happier men.

"Well, what do you want? I can't waste the whole morning," spoke the sullen man.

"Mr. Grump, won't you let the land in the Brook Strip remain as it is? We haven't as yet been able to find homes for more than one or two of the families that live there."

"Mr. Bear, you can go back to those people with my answer: NO! I informed every family living there that when a certain season came, namely, just before the first snow, it would be cleared and plowed. Now, have I made my plans more clear?"

"But, Mr. Grump, those families of little people will be homeless."

"Then let them move to the wild woods."

"But they are afraid of the wild places," returned Mr. Bear, "and the meadow is too open for safety."

"That is not my affair," muttered the farmer as he arose from his chair. Then he added, or started to add, "If that is all, Mr. Bear, I shall bid you good day," but the words remained unsaid, due to a strange occurrence.

When Mr. Bear began to talk about the small animal families, he stood, and began to walk back and forth across the room. He put his hand in his pocket and felt the Rainbow Stone, so he took it out and held it in his hand without thinking about what he was doing. He walked near the window in his agitation, and as he did so, a slant of sunlight shone through the stone. The sunlight sank deep, deep within the center, amid the many shining sides, and lingered there a moment, shimmering. Tiny rays floated out around the room, and as the small rainbows splashed around, somehow the room changed, and became more pleasant.

Farmer Grump had never felt quite so strange in all the time he could remember. There was warmth all around him, and it spread deep inside him. His mouth curved in a smile, and as soon as that happened, Farmer Grump felt better. Mr. Bear stood there, the stone in his hand, with little rainbows bouncing everywhere. He looked at Farmer Grump, who was suddenly smiling, and couldn't believe what he saw.

No one had ever seen Farmer Grump smile. It wasn't a very big smile, that first one, but the next was better, and soon they were just like the smiles you'd find on any happy person. Farmer Grump walked over to where Mr. Bear was standing, and looked right into the Rainbow Stone.

"Would you like to hold it?" asked Mr. Bear, for though he had never liked this man, still, he knew something extraordinary was happening and that the stone was helping to make it happen.

Farmer Grump took the stone carefully, gently, and held it in his hand, as he had seen Mr. Bear hold it. After looking down into the stone for a minute, he glanced up. Mr. Bear was so astonished, he sat down on a chair with a plump. What had happened? Farmer Grump didn't look the same at all. He had changed entirely, and in such a short time! The frown had

vanished completely, the down-drawn lines in his face were all turned up, and he was smiling broadly. He stood straighter, as though a weight had been lifted from his back.

Mr. Bear thought, "He's not a bad fellow at all. I wonder if he can play croquet?"

When Farmer Grump spoke it was in a soft kindly voice, which didn't surprise Mr. Bear, somehow. "This is a beautiful stone, Mr. Bear, beautiful. I don't believe I have ever seen anything so pleasing." He handed the Rainbow Stone back to Mr. Bear. "Mr. Bear, I may as well admit I don't have a single sound reason for wanting to plow the Brook Strip. I suppose I was just being what people think I am. Long ago, I got started being a mean old man, and I never could stop. Tell all the small animals they are safe in their present homes, and that I will remove the traps."

Mr. Bear bounced out of his chair. "Mr Grump, thank you, sir. I'm sure all the people in the county will declare a holiday in your honor. We have all been very worried."

Farmer Grump hung his head and looked sideways. He was embarrassed, but pleased. "No need for that, no need for that, at all. Should never have caused such trouble in the first place. You know, my real name is Gumple. Would you call me that?"

"Why, of course, Mr. Gumple. Very careless of me! I guess I never saw your name in written form," said Mr. Bear.

"I've been called Grump by everyone for years, but I hope that will change now," said Farmer Gumple.

Mr. Bear skipped toward the door. "Well, Mr. Gumple, I must be going to spread the news, but I wonder if you would care to come over to End O' the Lane for dinner tonight?"

"Mr. Bear, I would be wonderfully pleased, and perhaps I could have another look at your stone then, too?"

"Why, of course," said Mr. Bear. "We will expect you at six o'clock. Goodbye Mr. Gumple." He almost ran down the road, for he was eager to tell all the families that they had no reason to worry now.

Chapter 13
Crisis

The season began to turn to autumn and a sharpness came into the air. It touched the leaves each night and colors deepened in wood and meadow. Many of the bird families left for the southland. A lassitude gradually affected each member of the House at the End of the Lane. Chester couldn't get the phrasing of his latest poem to please him. Rabbit lost interest in seed catalogues. Miss Lucy, all prepared to paint, stared into the distance without lifting her brush. Bartholomew moped over the fading of his first garden. Mr. Bear, usually so staunch and cheerful, was actually morose. The family finally realized that his anxiety was at the heart of their distress.

He grew more and more worried as the days passed. He could be found standing in the garden, looking this way and that, with a most doleful expression. He would usually reach into his pocket for his Rainbow Stone, and look at it awhile. This would apparently make him feel better, for he would smile a little.

One night as dessert was finished, Mr. Bear spoke. "I hope you will not mind, but there is a very grave matter I must discuss with all of you. Could you all join me in the library?"

"Of course, Mr. Bear," said Miss Lucy, and she led the way into the book-filled room where the gold lettering made the darkened corners glint.

"Maybe we shall find out what is bothering poor Mr. Bear, and perhaps we can help him," she whispered to Mr. Rabbit.

"I certainly hope so," he replied, as he sat in his favorite green chair.

Mr. Bear began, "I had chosen not to tell you all this in hopes that the situation would change and make it unnecessary to worry you. I do not like to shock you. Now I have decided, finally, that you must be told, and that no way is easier than another . . ."

Miss Lucy was hopping in her chair by this time. "For goodness sakes, Mr. Bear, what ever is this all about? Tell us quickly! What is the trouble!"

Mr. Bear would not be rushed. "You may have heard that the Council wanted to put in a direct road to Fartowne which would save one and seven-eighths miles. Well, they have decided it shall be done. The measurements have been made, and the new road, as it is now planned, will take away our whole front yard."

When he stopped speaking there was a dull, gray silence. Then Mr. Rabbit spoke. "It is unheard of! We cannot allow it!"

"Our beautiful gardens!" Bartholomew was pale.

"What will become of the birds and the gold fish, and the bees?" Miss Lucy wanted to know.

This was indeed a terrible thing! No wonder Mr. Bear had been feeling bad, when this was heavy on his heart. What in the world could they do?

"There was one hope I had for some time," Mr. Bear continued. "There is another way the road could go, through open country, and be exactly the same length, but the plan was abandoned."

"Why didn't it go that way?" Chester inquired.

"There was one big hill in the pathway of the road, and it would have been expensive to buy. The council therefore decided that the road must go this way instead. Our land will be condemned, and used for the road. If we could buy the hill and give it to the Council, then they would approve that route."

"We haven't enough in the bank," answered Mr. Bear. "You see, I hoped we could, too, but our funds are inadequate. Now you all see how bad the situation is, and why I have been so worried."

Chester's eyes glowed, all black like coal buttons, and he said, "Somewhere on the desk is a piece of paper that will end our troubles!"

Of course, everyone looked up in great surprise. Was Chester trying to be funny at such a bad time? Mr. Bear didn't know what to think, and so he looked around at the desk, but he couldn't see anything unusual.

"There, there, on the left side, under the blotter," said Chester.

"My goodness! Where did you ever get such a check as this?"

"Mr. Thundergaard gave it to me."

"I thought he gave you a bronze plaque." Miss Lucy interposed.

"He did, but he gave me this, too."

"Why didn't you tell us?"

"I just forgot it," said Chester. "Is it enough to buy that hill, Mr. Bear?"

"Oh, yes, with a generous portion to spare!"

"Thank heaven for saving our home," said Miss Lucy. "This calls for a Special Occasion Cake!" So she went out to the kitchen and made a huge chocolate cake with white icing, thick with chopped pecans, that everyone enjoyed immensely.

Everyone discovered a new zest in life. The first snow fell, and plans were made for the greatest celebration of the year.

Chapter 14
Christmas at the House at the End of the Lane

Bartholomew bounced around the house in a veritable fret, waiting for Christmas. There were such preparations underway! Out in the kitchen Miss Lucy had been making cakes for a whole month. Each day Chester and Bartholomew shelled nuts to help, and chopped fruit, too, sometimes, in a large round wooden bowl, not forgetting to taste a tid-bit once in a while.

The house was full of all sorts of delightful aromas. There were warm, spicy cooking smells in the kitchen and dining room, while all the other rooms had the odor of pine and fir, for there were decorations everywhere. But the hall upstairs by Rabbit's room was very fragrant in a special way. No one could guess what it was, and Rabbit wouldn't tell. He was doing secret Christmas things.

Secret doings were going on all over the house, in fact: upstairs, downstairs, and in the basement, too. Paper rustled and crackled, ribbon whished and scissors snip-snapped as packages were wrapped and put away in hidden places, just waiting for *The Day*.

Bartholomew was wondering what Miss Lucy did every afternoon at three o'clock, for no matter where she was, or what she happened to be doing, she stopped and went to the kitchen. Bartholomew finally decided that since he had nothing particular to do this afternoon, he would just follow her down to the kitchen and watch Miss Lucy do whatever it was she was doing with such regularity.

"What are you doing?" asked Bartholomew.

"Well," said Miss Lucy, and her eyes were bright with fun, "this is a secret."

"Any special kind of secret?" Bartholomew wanted to know.

"Well," Miss Lucy explained, "this is preparation for a special Christmas thing we do each year, but just for fun, suppose we call it a Christmas secret and you see if you can guess what it is."

"That would be jolly, but am I smart enough to guess it?"

"Of course you are, and we shall give you clues to help. Oh, Mr. Bear, I'm glad you came in. Will you take this to the basement?" She handed Mr. Bear, who had just come into the room, a blue bowl full of a milky looking liquid. Bartholomew guessed there was sugar in it, because the sugar jar was out on the table, and open too.

"Are you trying to guess what this is, Bartholomew?" asked Mr. Bear.

"Well, yes, sir, I was."

"Bartholomew, ummm, let me see, perhaps I can give you a clue…ummm. Well, this is made of summertime things used in a wintertime way. There, does that help you?"

Bartholomew scratched behind his left ear, and little furrows waggled on his forehead. "Summertime things used in a wintertime way. No, that doesn't help at all."

Mr. Bear chuckled, and his eyes were as bright as Miss Lucy's when he spoke to her. "Perhaps you could give him a small hint, too, but only one, mind you."

"Of course, but I must have a moment to think of a good one. Let me see now. There are two kinds of things and I'll give you a clue to each one:

>'Oh I have great big eyes that do not see.
>I chase the dark with light so free.'

There, I've made a rhyme of my clues."

Bartholomew was obviously excited, for his ears were straight out, one right, the other left. He thought, and thought, but couldn't find one single fact that was the answer to both of the clues. "Could I have another clue?" asked the perplexed Kangaroo.

"I don't know why not, replied Mr. Bear. "But you had better wait until we have tea so you can ask Mr. Rabbit to give you one."

With this to look forward to, Bartholomew thought that tea time would never arrive. He stood on one foot, and then on the other. He walked to the window and looked out at the snow. He poked the kitchen fire and threw on another log. Finally, in desperation, he blurted out to Miss Lucy, who was sitting at the round table, reading, "Please Miss Lucy, may I fix the tea wagon?"

"Why, Bartholomew Kangaroo, are you so hungry as that?"

"No, ma'am, or rather, yes, ma'am. Well, I would like something to eat, but that can wait."

"If it can wait, why do you want to fix tea early?"

"It is just that I would so like to hear the clue Mr. Rabbit will give me and Mr. Bear said it would be given at tea time."

"Bless you, Bartholomew, there's no reason we can't hurry. I will help, and we shall have tea early. You get the cups and saucers, spoons and cream. I'll put on the kettle. There now. Here are some tarts."

"Would you like me to butter some bread, Miss Lucy?"

"Yes, thank you. You are a great help, always."

Bartholomew dropped his eyes, embarrassed at being praised, but he was mightily pleased, though all he said was, "Thank you. Is it time to sound the blue bell?"

The blue bell was used to call people to meals when everyone was already in the house, as they were in this freezing weather. It was made of cobalt blue glass dappled with silver flecks, and it was shaped like the flower campanula, and hung from a silver stem. When the stem shook, a tiny silver stamen inside the flower swung from side to side, making the happiest, most melodious tinkle.

"Yes, Bartholomew, ring it, if you please."

The lovely notes wended through the rooms, and up the stairs and under the doors, calling all to the kitchen for hot tea before the warm fire. When everyone was settled, Miss Lucy explained to Mr. Rabbit, "Bartholomew is trying to guess the secret that is in the basement. Mr. Bear and I have each given him a clue. 'Summertime things used in a wintertime way' was Mr. Bear's, and mine was:

> 'I have great big eyes that do not see,
> and I chase the dark with light so free.'

Now, will you give him one?"

"Oh, certainly, Bartholomew, I shall be glad to, but this has taken me unawares. I am, you might say, unprepared. However, if you will be kind enough to allow me a few moments for cogitation, I shall try to oblige." Bartholomew's eyes were so wide with amazement at this speech, the longest Mr. Rabbit had ever uttered, that they felt uncomfortable.

"Mr. Rabbit is reading again," explained Mr. Bear. "It is like this every winter. Sometimes he is most difficult to understand, like he was the winter he read Spenser."

"Oh, I see," said Bartholomew, but he didn't really. He only wanted Mr. Rabbit to hurry and give him the new hint. Bartholomew waited while Mr. Rabbit took his cup of tea, and stirred it with a small spoon. He waited while Mr. Rabbit ate two butter sandwiches, one tart, a piece of hot cake, and one and a half hot muffins.

Finally, as Mr. Rabbit handed his cup to Miss Lucy to be refilled, he spoke. "This surprise actually includes two things, acting as one. It is substituting one kind of thing for another, but with the same purpose. One half changes heat for coolness. That is my hint."

Bartholomew stood and looked at Mr. Rabbit, more puzzled now than ever, Mr. Bear chuckled, and Miss Lucy smiled. "There, that's something to think about for awhile, isn't it?" she asked.

"Yes, indeed, it is, and I'm going to keep trying to guess the answer, even if it seems to be getting difficult."

"Keep at it, my boy," encouraged Mr. Bear. "We will give you a new clue every day until Christmas, so you will have several more chances to guess the secret."

"This is a lovely game, and I know I shall be able to guess the answer soon." Bartholomew went into a corner to think about all the clues.

The next day was occupied in packing boxes, for gifts were to be delivered. These were mostly boxes of good things to eat. Tin boxes filled with citron bars and ginger curls; flat pasteboard boxes lined with rows of date delight and pecan surprises; small baskets heaped with fruit bars and butter cookies—delicious morsels, every one.

When the boxes, the baskets, and the tins were all filled, Bartholomew went to the library. He took down the encyclopedia volume printed "Sub-Tom," but there was nothing helpful to guessing the secret under "summertime." Then he looked under "eye" but that was no help, either, though it was very interesting to read. "Great big eyes that do not see," he said to himself, "what a puzzle this all is! There'll be a new hint today, at dinner time, though, and maybe I shall be able to guess when I hear it." Naturally he was glad when dinnertime arrived.

"Mr. Bear, Mr. Bear, are you ready to tell me the new clue?" Bartholomew wanted to know as soon as he entered the room. Everyone was smiling.

"For some reason, I have been overlooked in this game, but I prepared a clue for Bartholomew, anyway," said Chester.

"Good, good."

"Here it is, and it applies to both of the things.

'As cool and as bright as the moon;
Such beauty floats on the air.' "

Bartholomew murmured, "That is beautiful Chester," and was thereafter quiet for some time. He was busy running his mind around and between the clues he had.

The next day, Chester, Bartholomew, Rabbit and Mr. Bear loaded the wrapped packages on sleds, put on snow shoes, and trudged off to the star fork together. Sixteen roads met at the star fork, so each of the friends took a different road, and delivered the packages intended for those families who lived along that particular road.

Chester left those for the Wandreds, Scotts, Pembrokes, Johnsons, and the Bradshaws. Mr. Rabbit visited the Carters, Witherspoons, Dawsons, Rockmans, Dugdales and the Kentwillens. Meg's brother left presents at the Throckwells, Scalters, Punwins, Dubbins, Seatrolls and Jockens. Mr. Bear took the road that went through the village, so he had the gifts going to the postmaster, the apothecary, Mr. Thwaite the grocer, Mr. Blikens, and Alfred Stubbs the stationer. Bartholomew had some things to deliver to the families of small people who lived on Brook Strip, and he had an invitation to be delivered to Farmer Gumple.

As Bartholomew swung along on his snow shoes, he thought and thought and thought. He still couldn't guess the answer to the riddle. "Beauty like the moon . . . on the air," he muttered to himself. "Eyes that do not see . . . summertime things . . . Oh, here is the house," and he knocked on the door. It was soon opened by Farmer Gumple.

"Bartholomew! Come in, come in, you must be chilled."

"No, not at all, really. I've been to the Brook Strip with some packages, and for you there is this invitation from everyone at home. We would like you to spend Christmas with us."

"Well," stuttered Farmer Gumple, "I don't know what to say. After all, there is the stock to feed."

"One of Meg's brothers can do that for you quite easily."

"Do they really want me to come?" asked the farmer in a wistful voice.

"Indeed we do," (Bartholomew was so proud to say we). "The festivities will begin with lunch on Christmas Eve. You must spend the night, of course, so as to be there early on Christmas morning, when we will open our presents. Say you will come, Mr. Gumple."

"Mr. Kangaroo, I accept the splendid invitation with great delight, and I shall be there promptly for lunch on the day before Christmas."

"Good, good. Now I must hurry, so I can be home before dusk. Goodbye,

Mr. Gumple." Bartholomew went on down the path toward home swinging his arms. His feet were going plip-plop in the snowshoes, while he puzzled and puzzled. "As cool and as bright as the moon . . . what could it be? Well, dinner was not far away, and with it another hint."

Dinner on these snowswept evenings was cozy. Outside the trees scratched with icy claws at the windows, but the fire crackled within and cast a glow over everything. Bartholomew found it most difficult to wait until someone else remembered about the fresh clue, but Mr. Bear (kind Mr. Bear) saved his impatience.

"Well, Bartholomew, are you ready for the clue for today?"

"Oh, yes, sir. I thought today would never pass. I have been ready since yesterday."

"Is it my turn to supply it tonight, or is someone else ready?" Mr. Bear looked around the table at the smiling faces, but each in turn said no. "So be it then. This is part one: 'This light is free.' Now for a clue to the second thing: 'This is a flower's best friend.'"

After he had heard the new clue, Bartholomew said very little; he was busy thinking. He did remember to report on the delivery of the packages and to announce that Farmer Gumple had accepted the invitation. Everyone was pleased he was coming. There would be quite a party, for Mr. Stork, the Vicar and Mrs. Weatheree would be invited also.

"Why don't we all go together to the Vicar's and select a Christmas tree on the way home?" he suggested.

"Lovely idea," said Miss Lucy.

"Excellent," said Mr. Rabbit, and Chester and Bartholomew both agreed.

The next morning as soon as breakfast was over, there was a general fuss as they all put on warm clothes for the long walk in the crispy air. Mufflers were wrapped around throats, earmuffs fit snugly against tender ears, gloves found, and at Miss Lucy's suggestion, Bartholomew, who sometimes had cold feet, put on three pairs of socks. As the party was to go by way of the public road it wasn't necessary to wear snowshoes, but everyone carried them, hanging down in back, like strange webbed wings. Just before leaving, Miss Lucy gave each one a package to carry.

"Lunch," she said.

"Miss Lucy, you are a positive wonder," bowed Mr. Bear. "I had forgotten sustenance entirely. Thank you."

"We would never be able to accomplish much if Miss Lucy wasn't around to remember these things," said Mr. Rabbit.

"She is a very good nurse, too," Bartholomew was thinking.

"There's no occasion to which she isn't equal," Chester said.

Miss Lucy was happily snappish. "You all get along out the door, or we will never reach the Vicar's at all, much less find our tree."

"She's right, she's right, shall we go?" Mr. Bear was first to step out into the shining cold morning. It was so bright it was difficult to see anything at first, but as they walked to the tall gates and out into the lane they began to notice what a wonderful day it was.

They walked along, and talked pleasantly. Chester and Bartholomew went on ahead, and then were left behind as they had a rousing snow fight. Chester nearly won, but fell on an ice slick, and Bartholomew had his hat knocked awry. What a beautiful day this was, so polished and clean and clear. The snow reflected the sunlight, and the rays made small glinting patches of color everywhere. Everyone was happily discussing plans when suddenly Mr. Bear, who was familiar with the road, said, "Here is the last turning, and the Vicar's house is just three streets along in the village."

"We cannot possibly be here so soon," Miss Lucy stated.

Chester complained, "There's been only one snow fight, and Bartholomew won. It's not fair."

"Hold fast, hold fast," said Rabbit, chuckling. "There will be time enough for many fights on the way home. I alone will challenge the two of you."

"Ho, ho, what bravery! Couldn't you use a stout bear, for carrying snowballs at least? I'd enjoy getting in for a bit of the fun."

"If you want a battle, we shall be glad to oblige the two of you," returned Chester, and Bartholomew nodded approval.

By this time Miss Lucy had pulled the bell cord at the house and Mrs.

Weatheree answered.

"What a lovely surprise!" she exclaimed, when she saw everyone there. "Come in, come on in. Vicar, oh Vicar, we have company. Miss Lucy, everyone, take off your wraps, and come right into the dining room. There is a big fire there, and you shall have lunch shortly."

The Vicar came in as she was speaking. "Well, well, Miss Lucy, how do you do? Good to see you Mr. Bear, my friend . . . and Mr. Rabbit, Mr. Kangaroo, Chester Dog, sirs, welcome, welcome!"

Miss Lucy collected all the lunches, and followed Mrs. Weatheree into the kitchen to see if she could help in any way. Soon the ladies had the meal ready, and everyone sat down at the table. What a jolly time they had. There were large steaming bowls of rich sorrel soup, cheese biscuits fresh from the oven, and a light fluffy chocolate souffle, topped with hazelnuts. The lunches Miss Lucy packed supplied bread and butter, cheese, pecans and crunchy tart apples.

The Vicar and Mrs Weatheree accepted the invitation to visit, and plans were made for them to arrrive for the noon meal on Christmas Eve. "We really must be leaving," Mr. Bear said, and Miss Lucy agreed.

"We are going to stop in the wood and get our Christmas tree," explained Chester to the Vicar.

"Not before I have trounced you soundly in a fair snowball fight, with Mr. Bear's help," interposed Rabbit. The mufflers were again donned, mittens put on, ear muffs fitted, and soon, amid cheerful goodbyes from Mrs. Weatheree and the Vicar, the party set off again, bound for the woods to find the Christmas tree.

They followed the streets, then the high road as far as they could, but finally, when they were quite near to home, everyone fastened on the snow shoes, and prepared to cross the deep glinting drifts into the woods. Everyone, that is, except Miss Lucy, who declared that she would rather go on home.

"I will stop by Mr. Stork's and give him his invitation on the way. Be careful, all of you, and I shall have something hot ready for you by the time you reach home." She went off then, to Mr. Stork's, who was pleased to see her, and fixed her a cup of tea. When she asked him if he would like to join them for the holiday, he accepted happily. Later he walked Miss Lucy to the End-of-the-Lane.

No sooner had Miss Lucy left them, than the four comrades were in the midst of a rousing fight, snowballs flying and hats askew. Though the battle veered back and forth, in the end they all agreed breathlessly to call it a draw.

Cutting across the meadow in a long diagonal, Mr. Bear, Chester, Mr. Rabbit and Bartholomew were soon on the outer edges of the forest. Here they spread out like a fan in search of a good tree. They called back and forth to each other, so the woods rang gaily.

"A tree, a tree," Bartholomew squealed in his delight. He had found a perfectly shaped tree, one that could be cut down wisely, to the benefit of smaller trees smothered under the thick branches. "Come on, Mr. Rabbit, and measure it," he called, so Rabbit came and measured. Then he consulted with Mr. Bear, who added or multiplied some figures on a piece of paper.

"Exactly the proper height," he said. "What do you think of the proportion?" he inquired of Chester, who was acknowledged as the most artistic of them all.

"Fine, oh yes. Quite lovely, nice, just right," he said, as he walked around it, looking up, followed by the rest, until they formed a circle around the tree.

Later, when they were all drinking spiced cocoa in the kitchen at home, Bartholomew, who was still thinking over the Christmas secret, asked:

"What about the clue for today? Who is next with a hint?"

"Me," said Rabbit, "I am. Are you ready? It is in two parts, like the rest. 'All that gleams in the swamps at night is not foxfire,' and 'Birds are not the only creatures that fly.'"

The next day was the day before Christmas. What eagerness, and anticipation. Whispering and laughter all over the house and whisking things out of sight when someone unexpected walked by an open door, and last minute preparations, and much running up or down stairs. The house smelled so delicious, was so filled with laughter, and snatches of song and happiness, it was hard to imagine things getting better, but they did.

Farmer Gumple arrived with great bundles tucked in every pocket until he was almost round. He was pleased himself, and he brought a particular kind of glow with him.

"Happy holiday, happy holiday all! I am very glad you asked me to come over."

"Welcome, Mr. Gumple. I'll show you to your room," and Mr. Bear started toward the stairs, as Miss Lucy came from the kitchen.

"Hello, Farmer Gumple, glad you got here safely. As soon as you are ready, there's a cup of hot tea to warm you."

"Thank you kindly, Miss Lucy, I'll be right down." He followed Mr. Bear up the stairs, looking like a great brown knobby ball, the way the parcels stuck out all around him.

The door bell rang again, and there was Mr. Stork, his arms also full of brightly colored packages.

"Ho, Mr. Stork," shouted Bartholomew, whose ears had been sticking up since he awoke that morning. "Come in, come in. Isn't it wonderful?"

"What?" the dignified Mr. Stork wanted to know.

"Why, everything," explained Bartholomew. "Just everything."

"I agree, entirely," said Mr. Stork smiling.

Bartholomew smiled back, and said, "I'll show you to your room, and there's tea in the kitchen."

"Good, good, nothing better."

Before they could move, the bell rang again, and the Vicar and Mrs. Weatheree had arrived. The Vicar's glasses were frosted with the cold, and Mrs. Weatheree's cheerful voice rang throughout the hall. Soon the guests had been to their rooms, taken off their coats and hats, and had come downstairs again. There was a great babble and hum of voices. The Vicar and Mr. Bear discussed an essay by Charles Lamb. Farmer Gumple and Mr. Stork were arguing the relative merits of crop rotation. Miss Lucy and Mrs. Weatheree were arranging the bowl of fruit for luncheon, and Chester, Rabbit, and Bartholomew were finishing a game of darts in the corner. It was not long before lunch was ready, and everyone sat down to eat in high good spirits.

"Well, Bartholomew, have you guessed the Christmas secret yet?" the Vicar wanted to know, for he had been told the story by Mr. Bear.

"No, sir, I haven't, but then, I haven't had the last clue yet, either," and Bartholomew laughed merrily, for he was really no nearer the answer than he had been at first. He knew that, and everyone else knew it, but it was fun pretending.

"As soon as lunch is over," Mr. Bear spoke, "shall we put up the tree?"

"Good," said Mrs. Weatheree, "I'm so glad you haven't done it yet."

"What do we do then?" Bartholomew wanted to know.

"Then we put the packages around underneath," replied Chester, "and we sing and play music and games and have good things to eat."

Farmer Gumple was rather quiet, and Mr. Bear noticed, so he said, "Mr. Gumple, you are to be my special helper. You and I shall go down to the basement for the tree."

"Fine, fine, do we go now?" So off they went, and returned a little later with a great rustling and scraping, dragging the tree to the large parlor. Finally, when the tree was fixed firmly in a place satisfactory to everyone, they all paused, admiring the choice tree and sniffing the sharp acid odor of the needles. Up and up and up it towered, right to the ceiling. Green, full of straight bushy branches, the perfect tree!

"Never saw a prettier tree," said Farmer Gumple.

"Just magnificent," agreed the Vicar, as everyone else nodded affirmation.

"Come now, time to bring the packages down," said Miss Lucy.

"I'll race you to the top of the stairs," Chester challenged Bartholomew, and away they went with a clatter of feet, while the others followed at a more sedate pace. Bartholomew won by a hop and gathered the first armload.

There had been so many gifts to bring downstairs, to carry from the basement, or the kitchen, or wherever they had been hidden, that putting them under the tree took all afternoon.

When all the bundles and packages, parcels and boxes were under the tree, the floor was completely covered, obscuring the whole center of the room. What a tangle of reds and greens and blues and yellows, a tinkle of silver ribbon, and a jingle of gold. There were packages with bells, some with balls, and others with sprigs of fir, or small cones. There were packages of every shape. There were great, huge parcels, and some that were so small, so minute, that it was hard to see them at all.

After dinner, as everyone was going into the parlor, Bartholomew wanted to know, "Are we going to decorate the tree now?"

There were smiles from all but Farmer Gumple, who didn't know the Christmas secret. "No, Bartholomew, and that can be your last clue," Miss Lucy explained.

"Not any decorations at all?"

"There's not a single candle, nor one glass ball, no popcorn nor strings of cranberries, or anything like that."

Bartholomew thought this was very strange, but of course it was a beautiful tree. Still, it seemed so odd. But things always worked out so well here in this wonderful house that he certainly wasn't going to worry. He was too busy feeling good, thinking about the clues to the secret, and wondering if they believed in Santa Claus. No one had said anything about hanging stockings. Well, he could always sneak down and put his stocking up when everyone else was in bed, if that was necessary.

All the family and the guests were sitting quietly by this time, grouped around the fireplace, watching the faery castles in the flames. A peace and clear happiness was over all, and they sat silently in fellowship. The Vicar spoke of the reason for and the symbols of the loving celebration. After that, Chester told a beautiful Christmas story, and then each in turn told one. As the last story was finished, the music of the carolers was heard. They were invited in, of course, and everyone sang the gay joyous songs of the season. Then refreshments were handed round, amid laughter and conversation.

After the singers had gone, Mr. Bear spoke. "Mr. Stork, will you help me with the table? Mr. Gumple and you, Vicar, had better come along to carry the other things. We must hurry. It is very late, and it would never do for him to see us." So away they went.

Bartholomew whispered to Chester, "What and who are they talking about? Can it possibly be . . ." He hesitated, too shy to say it right out.

Chester helped his friend, "Yes, it is Santa Claus. You have been worried, haven't you? Of course he comes here."

"You see," Miss Lucy had been listening also, "this is his very last stop before his long trip homeward. We always fix a small supper, and put out slippers and a robe for Santa Claus, so he can relax a little, and warm up, before he goes back."

"Oh, how nice," said Bartholomew. "How very nice."

Soon Mr. Bear and his helpers returned. The table was fixed, a supper spread, an easy chair was placed close by, the kettle and slippers put on the hearth, and lastly, the stockings were hung (to the delight of Bartholomew, who thought it had been forgotten). All was ready.

Now the Vicar told the story of Bethlehem, and then everyone retired, taking the wonder of the story with them. The house was quiet. Outside, stars shone from a clear, cold sky, and glinted on the snowdrifts. The house was a shadow nestled in the snow.

Bartholomew knew he would not sleep, and Farmer Gumple didn't think he would, either, but they did. In the morning, everyone went downstairs together, but Bartholomew and Farmer Gumple were encouraged (even pushed) to enter the parlor ahead of the others.

"Oh!" was all that Bartholomew could manage to say.

"I never . . . I never thought such a thing could be," stammered Farmer Gumple.

"As beautiful as always," said Miss Lucy.

"Somehow I never quite remember how it is," said Mrs. Weatheree, and the Vicar intoned a pleased "Ah."

Bartholomew realized the meaning of all the clues at last. There were, indeed, none of the usual decorations. The tree was alight with glowworms and butterflies, summertime things. Strings, loops, and twinkling stars of shining fireflies (firelight), shimmered, and glittered, and blinked and twinkled until the great green tree seemed almost aflame with light. The butterflies (eyes that cannot see) were just as beautiful as ever! Large and small, swirling or sitting, they slowly opened and closed their wings. Wings of pearly blue, brilliant red, yellow, orange, and purple; irridescent hues, glinting in the light. Such splendor of color, such magnificence! Such a superb Christmas tree!

First they opened the gifts. Some were in their stockings, along with nuts, fruit, and confections. Others, too large to fit, were piled next to the fireplace, under a note of thanks from Santa for the welcome supper they had left him. There was a large crystal ball for Chester; a rare delicate Chinese fan for Miss Lucy; Farmer Gumple's gift was a silver Irish harp. He almost cried for happiness, it was so beautiful. Bartholomew was given a very rich looking harmonica that produced the sweetest notes when he blew it. Mr. Bear was pleased with a set of ebony and ivory dominoes.

"Oooooh, look, look," cried Rabbit. "Look what's hanging out of my stocking!" There was a great amount of dark material. It was very soft, and there seemed to be yards and yards of it.

"Why, Rabbit, that material is very handsome," said the Vicar, "but what is it?"

"I don't know, yet, I only hope . . . Oh, yes, it is, it is!" Mr. Rabbit swung to his shoulders a cape, a cape made for grand gestures, a cape to keep warm with, to look daring with, and to use for games.

"I've always wanted one." Rabbit was sheepish, but happy. "And now, at last, here it is."

"My gift won't come out!" wailed Mrs. Weatheree, so Mr. Bear helped and a long thin package emerged. "It has a gold handle," she told the rest as she unwrapped. "And lace—it's a parasol, from Paris!"

Mr. Stork didn't hear her, however, for he was sitting bemused as he looked through a very rare old edition of the plays of William Shakespeare.

The Vicar was untying the ribbon on an uncomfortably large square box.

"A new checker board?" hazarded Rabbit.

"I think it is eighteen white shirts," said Mrs. Weatheree.

Mr. Stork looked up long enough to declare, "There's no telling from the outside." But by this time the Vicar had unwrapped a box made of polished wood.

"Open it, open it," they cried. So he did, and what a surprise, for the box was brimful with puzzles, one from India, a block maze made in China, a Cretan labyrinth, writing puzzles, guessing ones, and ones to solve with manipulation.

"I'll wager my present is the jolliest one of all," said Vicar proudly, but Farmer Gumple twanged his harp in protest, while the rest objected in other ways.

"That is the end of the treasures from Santa Claus," Mr. Bear declared, "but there are many more." And certainly he was correct.

There were budded bulbs of white and yellow narcissi for the ladies from Bartholomew, and a twelve pound jar of lavender, grown by Rabbit, for Miss Lucy. Mr. Bear's present to her was an antique case containing a folding easel, and Chester had written her a story all in rhyme.

Miss Lucy had knitted mufflers and earmuffs for everyone, in different colors, with mittens to match, and Farmer Gumple was so pleased he put his on right away.

Mr. Bear was touched to find some honey labeled "Blue Amarian." "My special delight, Mr. Rabbit, and you thought about this in time to plant those flowers away last spring. So kind of you."

A cordovan leather eyeglass case was Bartholomew's present to Mr. Bear. There was special tea from Mr. Stork, an ivory letter opener from Chester. Mrs. Weatheree, Farmer Gumple, and the Vicar had given him handkerchiefs, a set of colored inks, and a penknife with mother-of-pearl handles.

"See what I have!" Bartholomew was unable to stay quiet any longer. "Chester gave me this lovely crystal vase for my room, and look, Miss Lucy, Farmer Gumple knew I liked balls, and here is this excellent India rubber one for bouncing. Rabbit has collected seeds for all kinds of herbs, so I can have the herb garden I wanted. Thank you all so much," and he beamed all around.

Chester was lying on a soft Persian rug from Mr. Bear, gazing into his crystal ball. The Chinese screen Bartholomew had found for him stood nearby, and the pot of growing bamboo from the Vicar rustled in strange contrast to the glimmering Christmas tree.

Such a perfect Christmas! What a good year it had been, how full of happiness. Bartholomew was thankful he had a family. Farmer Gumple was glad to have friends. Everyone was happy and grateful. They were the most contented and cheerful people in the length and breadth of the land. They were happy, as good folks are happy, with a happiness which grew and circled outward. From that house affection radiated to the village and countryside. Its peace, beauty and goodwill warmed and strengthened all it touched.

This book was
designed & printed
at The Green Tiger Press.
The text is Goudy Old Style
by Torrey Services of San Diego.
The color separations were done by
Photolitho, AG., of Zurich, Switzerland.

Maps